For Love of Mary Kate

Hazel Mc Intyre

Hazel Mc Intyre

M P

Moran Publications

First published in Ireland by **Moran Publications** 1996

© Copyright Hazel Mc Intyre 1996
Reprinted 1998

ISBN 0-9524426-5-5

Typeset: Stuart Clarke
Cover Illustration: James McLaughlin

Printed and bound in Ireland by: Browne printing Company
Letterkenny Co Donegal.

I would like to thank all my family and friends for their support and encouragement, particularly Jan Mc Guinness, Mary Mc Kinney, and Sean Beattie.

And to my husband Charles who is my inspiration, I would like to dedicate

For love of Mary Kate

with all my love and gratitude.

Contents

For Love of Mary Kate

Hazel Mc Intyre was born on a farm in the Inishowen peninsula of Co. Donegal in Ireland. After leaving school she moved to London where she became a nurse, before marrying husband Charles. They later moved back to Ireland, where they now live with their three children.

Her first book "Iron Wheels on Rocky Lanes" which vividly recalls her Donegal childhood was published in 1994 to an outstanding ovation from the critics.

Chapter 1

The Promise

When Sara Quinn rounded the bend of the narrow road she saw the convent at the top off the hill, the mist blurring its harsh grey outline. The big iron gate gave a reluctant creak as she pushed it open. She stood in the gateway for a few seconds to gain her composure, all the while her lips moved in silent prayer. "Dear Lord, please let the child be born safely," she whispered. Walking to the door she pulled the bell rope and waited. A young pale faced nun peered out at her from the dark interior.

"Can I help you?" she asked.

"I'm Sara Quinn. I've come to see my daughter Maura."

"Come in and I'll see if Mother will see you," she said nervously.

"There is no need for me to see the Mother Superior. Just take me to see my daughter. Has the baby been born?" Sara asked anxiously.

"You will have to see Mother. You can wait for her

in here," she replied, opening a door along the corridor.

Inside the sparsely furnished room Sara paced the floor nervously. Walking over to the small window overlooking the front gates, she watched a group of brown clad children walk past the gates with heads bent. A few paces behind them a young, somber looking nun stared straight ahead, Sara shuddered as she watched. "The orphans, poor wee souls," she said aloud. Just then the door opened behind her. Turning around, she was greeted by an elderly nun.

"I am Mother General. Sister tells me that you are the Quinn girl's mother."

"Is she all right. Has the baby been born yet?"

"Yes, the child is born and your daughter is fine. A girl was born this morning. Sit down Mrs. Quinn, we need to talk," she said showing her a chair in front of a big desk.

"Please," Sara asked anxiously, "can I see them?"

"You may see your daughter presently. But, before you go up I need to talk to you," she said. Again she pointed to the chair. Sitting down reluctantly, Sara met the cold gaze of the elderly individual seated opposite.

"Before you see your daughter, I have a few things that I must tell you. As you are no doubt aware, your husband was adamant that the child should be brought up by the Sisters in the orphanage. So, I don't want her to become attached to the infant. It will only make it harder when the time comes for parting."

Cold eyes stared back at Sara as she spoke. Again

she felt a shudder run down her spine, at the mention of the orphanage. The picture of the sad downcast, brown clad little bunch of humanity that she had just seen came back before her eyes.

"I'm trying to change my husband's mind about the orphanage. I want her to bring the child up herself. With our help of course," she added.

"Children brought up in the orphanage are fed, clothed and well instructed in their faith. And many of them enter the convent in adult life. I feel in many ways that they have a better start than they would otherwise have growing up ...under these circumstances. Anyhow, I very much doubt if your husband will change his mind."

"Well, we will see. Can I see them now?"

"You can see your daughter. But not the child. Your husband made the arrangements, and he was most insistent that you should not see the child."

Sara felt again the deep anger towards her husband, an anger that was all consuming. Smiling across at the nun to hide her feelings, she said, "he was angry then. But, he is coming to terms with it better now. He just needs a little more time," she said gently as she looked into the eyes of the woman opposite, hoping that her lies were convincing.

"Be that as it may. But until such times as I am given further instruction from him, I must obey his order." Once more their eyes met. The nun smiled a thin smile before she spoke again. "I will get one of the Sisters to take you to your daughter. Just wait here," she said from the doorway.

Alone again Sara tried to control the deep anger inside her. "Damn you anyway John Quinn. Why are you punishing us?" she mouthed to the silent room. When Maura told her that Seamus, her cousin and neighbour had repeatedly molested her, she thought that her anger had reached its peak. Then when she tried to tell her husband John and he refused to believe her that anger spilled over to breaking point. The memory of his hateful words still rang in her ear. "Don't lie to me. Seamus is my own flesh and blood, he never laid a hand on her. She will never put a foot inside this door again. She has brought disgrace on me and all belonging to me," he had shouted repeatedly at her. But now she must control her anger as she waited to see her daughter, somehow she must try to bring comfort to her only child, whose whole world had been torn apart at the tender age of sixteen. How could she tell her that her father refused to allow her name to be mentioned as though she had never existed, and that she had to lie about coming here today? She knew that she couldn't tell her this; she had suffered enough already.

From her position on the bed Maura Quinn watched the young nun as she bathed her new- born infant. She had spent hours alone in an agonisingly painful labour, and now she felt drained of all emotion. The baby's cry seemed to come from a great distance while she watched, as if she were somehow an observer looking on from a distant place. Then suddenly the child was placed in her arms. She stared down at the tiny perfect creature, then she saw her bottom lip tremble, and in that instant a rush of unexpected love flooded through her. "I will call you Mary Kate," she said gently.

"She's hungry," the nun said stiffly as she put her to her breast. "You can feed her yourself for the first few days. It will give her a better chance of survival. But after that you leave her in our care," she added. "We don't want you getting attached to her, under the circumstances." She cleared her throat nervously and walked from the room.

Alone Maura gazed at her new born daughter with a mixture of wonder, love and pity. She was mystified as to how a perfect little being like this could have come out of such a hateful union of fear and blackmail. "I have nothing to offer you, nothing," she whispered. The door suddenly burst open.

"You have a visitor downstairs. I will take the child," the nun said breathlessly.

"Please don't take her away."

"It's orders, she is not allowed to stay. I will take her back at feeding time." From the doorway she looked back at Maura with a small tolerant smile.

"You are so young, please do as I say and forget about this wee one. To get attached will only cause you more grief. Just pray that the good Lord will help you to forget."

Five minutes later the familiar face of her mother

came into focus as she bent over her. The familiar comfort of her mother's arms filled Maura with that special feeling of security that had so often soothed her worst fears in childhood.

"The baby is so tiny and helpless, and so lovely." Her muffled voice sounded in Sara's ears.

"I want to go home with you, and take wee Mary Kate with me. The nuns keep telling me not to get attached to her. They say she will be taken to the orphanage." Her voice shook with sobs, and Sara felt a sharp pain rush through her. "Will he let me come home yet?" she asked. Freeing herself from her mother's embrace she looked into her eyes. "Will he?" she asked again.

"Not yet love. But I'm still working on it."

"He still doesn't believe me then," she said with a quiver in her voice. Sara shook her head slowly.

"I haven't given up. He's a stubborn man, your father. But he'll come round." Sara's words sounded hollow in her own ears, for in her heart she knew that she could never persuade him to allow his daughter to come home with her child. She hoped the encouraging smile she gave her, hid her true feeling of sorrow and despair. All too soon it was time to say their farewells. "I will be back soon, very soon," Sara said gently.

"Please beg him to let us come home." Her voice broke. "He must believe it wasn't my fault."

"I will try. Don't worry, leave it to me. I will think

of something," Sara said with a smile of encouragement.

Outside, the mist was beginning to clear. Sara stood looking back at the convent, but the weak sunlight failed to add warmth to its grey walls. A fitful wind smelling of rain made the tall trees shiver and whisper quietly, like cold old men. Sara shivered, then walked with heavy steps down the bray towards the station. .

Three days after her mother's visit Maura was moved to a small room at the other side of the convent. The nuns had stopped bringing the baby to her to be fed. As she stared at the crucifix on the opposite wall, she felt sure that she could faintly hear Mary Kate's cry. The sudden loud voice of Sister Mary coming from the other side of the door made her jump.

"Mother wants to see you now," she said poking her head around the door. "Come, I'll take you down to her. Maura stood up unsteadily.

"What does she want me for?"

"Well I'm not.. er.. allowed to say," she said, sounding nervous.

As she followed Sister Mary down the stairs she wondered what lay behind the sudden summons to see the Mother General. More than anything else she wanted to go home with her baby. Try as she might, she could not remember how long it had been since her father left her here. The nuns had for the most part treated her with cold indifference; it was almost as if they were afraid to show her any affection. When they reached the bottom of the stairs they both stood at the Mother's door. A thin smile formed on the nun's lips as she knocked.

"Come in."

"I've brought Maura Quinn, Mother. Will you be needing me again?" she asked.

"Yes, Sister, I'll call you when it's time," she added, nodding at her. "Sit down here, I have something important to tell you, about your future." She pointed to the chair in front of the big desk. Maura walked over and sat down apprehensively. Across the desk the elderly nun looked at her for a few moments, then clearing her throat she broke the silence. "Your father came here a few days ago to discuss your future" she began. "A decision was made, which I am now going to tell you about." Maura waited without taking her eyes from her face. "I have a boat ticket that your father bought for you. A single ticket to New York. The passenger ship leaves on this afternoon's tide, so you see there is no time to lose in getting your belongings together," she looked Maura straight in the face, showing no emotion.

"But my baby! I can't go without her, and I must see my mother first. Why did you wait until now to tell me this?" her voice shook with emotion as she struggled to keep back her tears.

"We decided it was best to wait until now to tell you, as I rightly guessed your hysterical reaction. You are very lucky that the good Lord has seen fit to give you a new beginning my girl, and as for the baby, you know that it is out of the question to even, think about taking the baby with you." She began pacing up and down behind the desk as she spoke. "Thank God the baby will be looked after, and you can began a new life, and maybe, in time the good Lord will forgive you ...for all this." She stopped pacing and accusingly waved her finger in Maura's direction.

Seated between two of the middle aged Sisters, Maura was driven to the quayside where the steamer was docked. With one Sister at each side of her, she was escorted towards the gang-plank. Then one of the Sisters went on ahead with the ticket in her hand. When they started to climb on board, she heard a familiar voice. Her heart leapt for joy, and within seconds she was in her mother's arms, laughing and crying all at the one time.

"The receipt for your ticket fell out of his pocket. Only for that, I wouldn't have known where you had gone." The nun became flustered and agitated, as she clung on to Maura's arm.

"Come on, it's time you were on board. We have to see you to your cabin as we were instructed," she called above the noise.

"It's all right. I will look after your baby until you get home again. Please love. Don't cry. Write to me as soon as you arrive. Send the letters to Ballyneely, care of Molly," her mother whispered in her ear, in her familiar soothing voice.

"I don't want to leave my baby. I don't want to go" she sobbed. Then she was tugged away from her mother's arms with the assistance of the second nun who had suddenly reappeared. When they reached the top of the gangplank, she looked down at the busy dock for her mother, but she had lost sight of her.

"Come on child, we have to find your cabin yet," one of the nuns said crossly. When on board the gentler of the two nuns, asked one of the Stewards for directions to the cabin, and Maura was led stumbling along narrow corridors, and down staircase, after staircase to the bowel of the ship. They reached the cabin at last, and one of the nuns opened the door. The interior was small and poky, two bunk beds and a wash basin summed up the furnishings. A battered trunk sat on the floor.

"It looks like your cabin companion has already been here. Sister and I will leave you now, we will wait at the bottom of the gang-plank until you sail". The gentler of the nuns turned back and kissed her on the cheek.

"God bless you child," she said before closing the cabin door.

Left alone Maura sat stiffly on the edge of the bunk, her thoughts running wildly around in her head. Suddenly she ran for the door, in panic she scurried along corridors and up flights of stairs. "Please God let her still be there" she panted as she at last reached the deck. A huddled mass of passengers pressed against the rails of the middle deck, it was impossible for her to see beyond the backs of their heads. In desperation she ran towards the stairway leading to the upper deck. As she began climbing the stairs a steward blocked her way.

"Sorry Miss, first class passengers only," he said.

Back on the middle deck, she pushed her way to the front. She looked down desperately trying to catch a glimpse of her mother. The ship was already moving away from the quay, making it harder to distinguish one face from another. On the quayside she could see handkerchiefs fluttering like moths in the yellow evening light. Tears blinded her eyes, as she made her way back down to the cabin. When she opened the door, a young dark haired girl sat on the top bunk, her eyes red and swollen from crying.

"Hello, I'm Hannah Mc Laughlin. We will be seeing a lot of one another for the next three weeks or so. I hope you don't snore," she said with a grin. "I know your name already, I saw it on the label of your trunk. Your Maura Quinn," she added.

"Hello Hannah, I'm glad to meet you," Maura said in a low strained voice. Taking a long look at her cabin companion, Hannah noted the brown eyes that seemed too large for her pale face, and the brown frock that hung over her skinny frame. 'My mother would never have allowed me to go to America if I looked as pale and skinny as she does. But, she could be pretty, even beautiful if she wasn't so pale and delicate,' she thought to herself. Then she asked.

"I'm going back out on the deck. Do you want to come?"

"No, but thanks, I'll just lie down for a wee while, I have a headache," Maura answered.

"See you later then. I want to see the last sight of the land. My brothers and sisters said they would watch the ship, from Clonmore hill".

When the door closed, she lay alone and bewildered, the throb of the engine reminding her that she was moving unwillingly further away from all that she knew and loved.

Maura lay on her bunk staring at the small porthole in the stuffy cabin. The ship lurched and tossed on the restless sea.

Hannah's head hung down over the top bunk clutching her rosary beads tightly and praying loudly above the noise of the storm. She had not anticipated the fury of an Atlantic storm, when she decided to emigrate, to America. "There is a good demand for dressmakers in New York," Aunt Mary had assured her in her letter. As the ship heaved and tossed, she thought she would not survive to see either New York or Aunt Mary. In her terror, she was sure that the ship would sink.

Maura lying in the bunk below felt no such panic. Her only prayers were for Mary Kate. She longed to hug her once more, and to feel her tiny hand clasp her finger. These were precious memories of the stolen moments she had spent with her in the convent nursery. "I didn't expect to love you Mary Kate," she whispered to herself, making no attempt to wipe away her tears.

"Thank God we are still alive, the storm is over," Hannah's shouts woke Maura from a heavy doze. Her head hung over the top bunk, her rosary beads dangling a few inches from Maura's face. "I must get my clothes on quick, and go and see if there is any damage." She jumped down from her bunk in one leap.

Maura smiled to herself at her new found friend's energy and optimistic approach to life. Meeting Hannah had made life worth living again for Maura. She shuddered at the memory of her second night on board when she almost ended it all. Looking into the dark waters, it seemed the only answer to her pain. She had stood gazing into the dark water for what seemed like an eternity, her mind had become calm, almost a hypnotic state, when Hannah voice came from behind her.

"What are you doing? God it's freezing out here, you will catch your death." When she made no reply, and she caught sight of one foot on the middle rail, the horror of what Maura was contemplating dawned on Hannah. She grabbed her by the shoulders, then forced her back until her two feet were firmly on the deck. She struggled but Hannah's physical strength overcame her resistance.

"For God sake Maura! Tell me I've got it wrong, you weren't thinking of ...." Hannah's voice trailed off.

"What if I was? Just leave me alone and mind your

own business. Why did you stop me?" She broke into hysterical sobs, while Hannah continued to hold her in a tight grip.

"Sure, it broke my heart leaving my home and my family too, but I had to go. I will be able to help them at home, when I get a job and can send some money, and so will you. It will be alright, you'll see, and into the bargain, there is your immortal soul to think about," Hannah's voice went on relentlessly, rocking Maura back and fourth, still holding her in a vice like grip. Hannah's voice, firm and kind slowly penetrated Maura's troubled mind, gradually her sobbing ceased. Hannah loosened her tight grip "Do you want to tell me about it? Come on down to the cabin and we'll talk, that's if you want to tell me." Not waiting for a reply she slowly guided Maura down the steps to the cabin. Hannah wondered again why fate had decided that she should have been chosen to share a cabin with this strange unhappy girl. She remembered seeing her for the first time the day they sailed. At first she noticed the grim faced nun holding the arm of the pale faced girl as they began climbing on board. Then she saw an older woman run towards them, they threw their arms around one another. The nun looked angry and tried to prise them apart, looking around her wildly as if, she was trying to summons help. Hannah had viewed this scene from the deck only now understanding its significance as Maura's sad tale slowly unravelled.

Chapter 2

The Parting

W hen Sara reached the age of nineteen she moved to the small remote farm in the townland of Clougher after her marriage to John Quinn. Her married life soon settled into a routine of hard work as the wife of a farmer.

When she produced a daughter two years after her marriage, for Sara her daily grind became worthwhile

But now with her daughter taken away from her, her whole life was in tattered shreds. By sheer chance she had found the receipt for the ticket to New York. He had intended to deport his only child without even telling her. Had that piece of paper not fallen out of his pocket she wouldn't even have had the chance to say good-bye to her.

As she stood on the hillside and watched the ship slowly disappear from her sight around the headland, tears ran down her cheeks, and her body shook with sobs as she slowly sank to the ground behind the dry stone wall.

"Maura, Maura," she repeated between sobs. Gradually she became still, as she felt her strength return when she thought of her granddaughter. "Mary Kate you are not going to rot away in some orphanage, I will make sure of that. He won't win this one," she said aloud.

As she stared out at the empty sea a plan began to take shape in her head. She hated herself for her past weakness. "Why did I allow a selfish bully to dominate my life for all these years? Was it easier to give way to him than to struggle against his dominance of me?" she asked herself out loud. "Had it taken the grief of parting with her only child to force her to face up to her own weakness?" Standing up she dusted herself, down and with head held high she marched down the hill to do battle.

There he sat, at the head of the table, when she walked through the kitchen door. Without glancing in his direction she filled the kettle and hung it on the crook, then she sat down opposite him and broke the silence.

"I'm going to the convent tomorrow to collect my granddaughter, and neither you or anyone else is going to stop me." His eyes narrowed with anger as he stared back at her in silence for a few seconds.

"Well are we now?" the mock sarcasm in his voice only renewed Sara's anger and determination. "No bastard offspring is coming into this house," he shouted scraping the legs of the chair on the floor as he stood up. Jumping up from her chair Sara looked him straight in the eye, "If my granddaughter can't have a home here then neither can I."

"Such brave words from a weak woman, and more to

the point, you have nowhere to go. Who would want you, not to mention the bastard?" he shouted.

"My only intention is to get as far away from you as possible," her voice came in low tones of disdain.

"Away you go then woman, and see how long you will stay," his hateful laugh echoed in her ears long after he had left the kitchen.

With relief she watched him walk towards the fields with a spade on his shoulder. Five minutes later she walked up the loft steps. 'Please let me find it' she prayed silently. Many a night she heard him climb these steps on returning from the market, and she was almost certain that this was where he hid the money.

Half an hour later she was still searching, keeping an eye on the loft door in case he came back early. Exhausted she sat down on the hay almost defeated, when her eye caught sight of a stone that looked shinier and smoother than the rest. Prodding it she felt it move, another push and out it came in her hands. Then feeling inside her hand rested on a hard object, and with a bit of manoeuvring a wooden box emerged from the dark hole. She opened it with shaking hands, and found it stuffed full of notes, counting out twenty pounds, she carefully put it back, and descended the steps.

Ten minutes later, suitcase packed, she stood in the kitchen gazing at the familiarity of it all. In the mirror above the chest she found herself staring at her own reflection, the deep set brown eyes stared back at her as she pinned the stray strands of auburn hair, tinged with grey at the temples, back into their place at the nape of her neck. Then she was on her way, not giving the house a second glance.

On the convent steps with her heart thundering in her ears, she took a deep breath before pulling the bell rope. 'Dear God help me to lie convincingly,' she silently whispered. At last the heavy door opened with a reluctant squeak.

"I'm Sara Quinn," she told the young nun standing in the doorway. Could I have a word with Mother General?" Seated in front of the stern faced Mother General, Sara summonsed up all her courage and began.

Only when the infant was in her arms did she accept her success. "She believed me, she really thought he had changed his mind about you, Mary Kate," she whispered sitting down at the side of the road, a safe distance from the big grey convent.

Looking down at the tiny baby that she had gladly given up her home for she spoke aloud, "It won't be easy, but I will always love you." Her tiny hand closed around Sara's finger, and in that moment a great love was born.

She walked about two miles before sitting down to rest again, when she heard the rumble of a horse and cart in the distance. She stood up as it approached.

"Where are you heading for?" the driver asked.

"Would you be going anywhere near Ballyneely?"

"Aye, going part of the way, as far as the cross-roads." he replied, then jumping down he helped her into the cart.

The cart ride gave her, a much needed rest, and the time to feed Mary Kate with the bottle of milk the young nun had given her. By the time they reached the rectory driveway dusk was falling. Cuddling the fretful infant close she shuddered as fear gripped her. 'I must be mad to throw myself on the mercy of a complete stranger. What if he turns us away?'

In the dull evening light she stood gazing at the old grey house that had once been so familiar to her. Then with gritted teeth she walked to the back door and gave a loud knock. From deep within she heard a dog bark, then Molly Sheehey's familiar voice called out.

"Who's there?"

"It's me, Sara," she shouted back. The door opened with a loud creak.

"Is it really you?" Molly's old face peered at her anxiously. "You are the last person I expected to see. Come in, come in," she repeated, opening the door wider. Sara noticed her slow shuffling movements, her bent spine and her general feebleness.

What a far cry from the strong agile woman she remembered from twenty years ago. When they were seated Sara looked around the once familiar kitchen; it had an air of neglect and drabness about it.

"I need your help Molly. It's a long story, which can

wait a while, but in short I need a job and a roof over my head for Mary Kate and me. She is my granddaughter you know," she added. Molly filled the kettle before answering.

"You and I go back a long way and you know I'll help you if I can." Sitting down again she tried to poke some life into the smoldering fire, before she went on.

"Things are bad here, aye damned bad. He is drunk out. He doesn't seem to care if the sun rises or sets anymore since the Misses died in childbirth, Lord have mercy on her. He blamed himself you see, and just went from bad to worse ever since," she shook her head slowly and, gazed into the fire with a look of despair before going on. "I don't believe he has a penny left, all drunk. Never leaves the bottle alone," her sad eyes looked back at Sara in the dim gloomy light.

"I won't ask for pay, all I want is a roof over our heads," Molly got stiffly to her feet.

"Well in that case up you go now and get it over with. Might as well face the lion in his den now," she added, nodding her head in the direction of the upstairs study. Sara followed her into the cold dark hall. "It's up there. Second door on the right. I don't like having to climb the stairs anymore than I have to," she added in a whisper. Grabbing Sara's hand she squeezed it, "I'll be praying for you, and me for that matter. God knows I need you," with that she headed back towards the kitchen cradling the infant in her arms.

A small ray of light shone from under the study door. Taking a deep breath she knocked and waited. She could hear faint grunting sounds from within. She knocked again louder.

"Who is it? Come in." When she opened the door she saw him slumped in a leather chair. The room was a complete shambles; books were strewn everywhere, the hearth rug almost invisible with a thick layer of dust and ashes. She remembered how hard she had to work in the old days to keep this most sacred retreat spotlessly clean.

"Who are you woman? What do you want?" he asked in obvious annoyance, while his bleary eyes peered at her suspiciously.

"I'm Sara Quinn. I used to work here many years ago before I got married. I was Sara Maloney then," she said her heart pounding in her ears.

"Well, what do you want," he asked again.

"I have a proposition to put to you Mr. Thompson," she answered, trying to sound more confident than she felt.

"All I ask is that you listen to me for a few minutes, and then you can make your decision." He made no reply, instead he pointed to the chair opposite him and indicated for her to sit down. Sitting down she cleared her throat and began. He listened passively without comment. Apart from an occasional frown he showed no emotion until she mentioned her grandchild. He got up from his chair and paced the floor for a few minutes, then turning around to face her again he asked.

"How old are you?"

"I'm thirty nine."

"You're young enough to be a grandmother. Did I hear you say you will work without wages?" She nodded. His blue-grey eyes stared at her for what seemed like an age before he spoke again. "If I agree, I might have to contend with that swine of a husband of yours one dark night. What guarantee can you give me of that, eh?"

"He won't come here, I guarantee that. "If you agree I promise you won't regret it. And I'm a hard worker, I've had plenty of practice... , God knows I have," she added.

He stared at her again, while twisting the fair, greying curls at the nape of his neck around the fingers of his right hand. Sara self-consciously averted her eyes from his fixed gaze.

"Very well then I'll give you six months trial, and if it doesn't work, out you go," he added with a gesture of dismissal.

She crept into bed in a state of both relief and exhaustion, the bed felt damp and smelled of must and neglect. She found it hard to come to terms with the changes in the house since her time working as a maid for Mr. Thompson's late uncle, who was the rector. It squeaked with order and cleanliness; what a far cry from the damp neglected house of today. As she lay in the musty bed Sara's thoughts ran around in circles. Molly had painted a depressing picture of how desperate things had become.   The farm was in such a state of neglect that it produced next to nothing to support them. Henry Mc Laughlin who had worked at the rectory as a farm hand for thirty years, had given up after two years without pay. As a result, there had been no turf saved for the winter; the only remaining cows were barren, and they had to buy milk. Molly herself had not been paid any wages in almost a year. "If I had any family or a home to go to I would have been gone long ago," she had concluded with a sigh. Mary Kate slept fitfully, as Sara pondered her dilemma, her fears for the future seemed to ooze out of the damp walls like dark ghosts. At last she fell into a restless sleep.

Molly was up and had the fire alight when Sara came into the kitchen. "I'm that glad to see you... I'm that glad," her old face broke into a broad smile of pleasure and relief as she spoke. "I was just about to give up and resign myself to the workhouse when you came along. And to make things worse, it gets harder, and harder to get up and down those stairs."

"Why can't you sleep on the ground floor? It's stupid, you having to climb all the way up to the garret when the house is nearly empty. What about the wee music room?"

"That would be grand. Do you think you could manage to get my bed and things downstairs?"

"I'll manage, but I'll have to wait to get him out of the house first." Just then the bell jangled ending their discussion.

The bedroom smelled of stale sweat and whiskey when Sara opened the door. His voice sounded thick and slurred as he spoke. "Get me some hot water, and then bring me some tea," he barked from the four poster bed, piled high with a jumbled heap of blankets and quilts.

"Very well Mr. Thompson," she replied turning to go.

"Oh, before you go, you can clean this room up a bit later. But mind you leave everything in its place."

"Very well," she added closing the door.

With a sigh of relief they heard his horse leave the yard about an hour later. "He is an even worse case than I thought. He knows how to give orders mind you, and on my first morning too," Sara said, as she gathered what cleaning materials she could find.

Molly looked lovingly at the infant on her lap, before settling her gaze on Sara again. "His bark is worse than his bite you know. Aye he wouldn't be so bad if it wasn't for the cursed drink. He just can't leave it alone. He would have been a different man if the Misses had lived." She shook her head and looked out the window, then her gaze slowly moved back to Sara with an expression of deep sadness, as if she were pleading with her to understand.

Molly looked after Mary Kate while Sara cleaned. Baby care was new to her, but she was learning fast. She was delighted to be able to sit down while she nursed, fed, and changed her without feeling guilty. While Sara worked she sang lullabies to her, remembered somewhere from her childhood, long ago.

Upstairs Sara scrubbed the floor of Mr. Thompson's room on her hands and knees. When she had finished the cleaning, she went in search of clean bed linen. The linen cupboard was in the same place, but the contents were damp and moth-eaten. "Is everything in this damned house rotten," she shouted to the empty landing in frustration, as she picked out the best of the linen for the wash. Along the corridor she opened the doors and windows of the bedrooms in turn. Spiders scurried for cover at the shock of sudden exposure to light and air. The nursery door stood at the end of the landing, she pushed open the door and stood looking around the interior for a few seconds. A rocking horse stood forlornly in the corner, its cobwebs swaying in the draught from the door. There was a faint pleasant scent in the air; somehow the room seemed to have escaped the worst of the damp that bedevilled the rest of the house. Walking over to the chest of drawers in the corner, she opened the top one and removed the layer of brown paper, then she examined the tiny garments with amazement. They were all in perfect condition, and sandwiched between each layer, a still scented bag of lavender.

Sara could sense the woman who had obviously so lovingly made them, her presence seemed to surround everything in the room; a peaceful friendly presence Sara thought. She opened the window and stood looking out, she watched the waves gently lapping on the rocks far below, the sea gulls swooped and dived low under the ragged cliffs. Turning back to the room, she surveyed it, and again she thought about the woman, who had made the beautiful baby clothes, as she happily awaited the birth of her first born. Sara again sensed her nearness, and she somehow knew that she had been happy in this room. "Oh, how different it might all have been for you and for me," she said aloud to the empty room.

A sudden noise interrupted her thoughts. She swung around in panic. He stood in the doorway staring at her with a strange troubled expression on his face.

"You scared the wits out of me Mr. Thompson," she said almost in a whisper, putting her hand to her pounding heart.

"Sorry, I didn't mean to scare you," he said with a hint of a smile. Much to her surprise he appeared to be sober, and he had shaved. As if reading her thoughts he said. "Molly probably told you I would be spending the day propping up Murphy's bar," he grinned at her before going over to the window. He seemed to stare out the window with unseeing eyes for an age before he spoke again. "Would you sort out a few of my clothes, and pack them for me? I'm going away for a few days." Suddenly he swung around to face her with a strange wild expression. "I see you have opened windows all over the place. The master bedroom is locked, and I want it to stay that way, do you hear? His eyes had a glazed stare, and for a split second, Sara thought he was going to strike her, then just as suddenly, the anger left him. "It's a far cry from the house you remember, eh? A bit of a shambles. I am willing to bet that you are sorry that you decided to make this your refuge," he turned towards the door, then swung back to face her. "Oh, by the way, do you think you could manage to drive the pony and trap back for me from the station tomorrow?"

"Aye, I could manage that." At the door he turned around again. "If there is anything in here that might be useful for the..er..child, take it, it will only rot like everything else."

"Thank you, thank you very much. And one more thing Mr. Thompson before you go," she added. "Would it be all right if we slept in here? It doesn't seem to be as damp as the room we are in now."

"I can't see why not. But remember I don't want a screeching child disturbing my nights."

"I'll see to that Mr. Thompson, thank you again." She watched him go with a mixture of pity and fear.

Chapter 3

A Rude Awakening

John Quinn watched the dawn break through the gap in the curtains with relief. His teeth chattered as he eased his body out of bed, while his breath came in painful gasps with each movement. Thirst drove him on slowly towards the kitchen. He lifted the water bucket from the table only to find it empty. Tears stung his eyes, and a long string of curses escaped his lips. "Dear God how will I make it to the well in this condition? I must get water, I must try," his own voice sounded distant in his ringing ears. He clumsily pulled on his coat, and opened the door. The cold damp air almost took his breath away, he shivered as he propped himself upright against the door jam. He took a few unsteady steps, before falling down on his face, the wind catching the bucket, and blowing it across the yard. He crawled back to the shelter of the doorway on all fours totally exhausted. Then he saw a figure walking up the lane, her head just visible above the hawthorn hedge. In desperation he yelled, "help... help," he yelled again above the noise of the wind. Ellen Murphy on her way to school turned her head just in time to see him. He beckoned with his arms, and then with relief he saw her walking towards him.

"What's wrong?" she asked.

"I've got a fever of some kind, water, I need water," he gasped. "For God sake hurry, don't just stand there. And then go and get Seamus," he urged between gasps.

He made his way back to bed on his hands and knees, and just managed to gather enough strength to pull the tangled mass of blankets around his shivering body.

A few minutes later Ellen brought him a mug of water, and he drank it greedily. "Seamus is not in, I knocked and shouted but there was no answer. I'll get help for you, don't worry." With that, she ran out the door before he could stop her.

Grace Murphy's voice startled him as she bent over him. "You're boiling up John, you need a doctor." He shook his head, "No, no doctor." Ignoring his protests, she went to the kitchen, and he could hear her giving Ellen instructions to go for the priest and doctor. He felt too weak to protest, and had to resign himself to his fate while he prayed for a quick end. He lay shivering and snivelling like a frightened child, tears of self-pity running unchecked down his face. "I don't want any truck with neighbours. Where the hell are you Seamus?" he muttered to himself. Almost before he knew it the room became a hive of activity, and he could only watch helplessly from under his mountain of blankets and old coats. He became painfully aware of his unshaven face and unwashed body, and he couldn't remember when he last changed the bed linen; probably not since she left. "Dear God how I hate them to see me like this." Tears again stung his eyes, as he helplessly turned his head to avoid their eyes. He watched Grace set a basin of water on the bedside table, and put the towel and soap beside it.

"I'll have you cleaned up in no time, it will make you feel better when it's done." She continued talking to him in a soothing, almost childlike fashion as she worked. Beginning with his face and hands, she washed up and down his body with brisk efficiency, always leaving the blankets in the middle to avoid his embarrassment.

"There now, doesn't that feel better?" she asked, pulling a clean night-shirt over his head. Then she brought clean sheets, turning him from side to side, she changed his soiled sheets. "There now, does that feel better?" she asked, getting up onto the bed on her knees, and lifting him up high on the clean pillows. This time his eyes filled with tears of gratitude.

"Thank you, thank you," he repeated. He dozed and hallucinated throughout the day.

Ellen Murphy sat by his bedside mopping his brow with a damp cloth, as the shivering was replaced by profuse sweating. He was periodically aware of Ellen's presence, and he was aware that he had been given the last rites. He had heard the words, phenomena, fever, crisis, the words were jumbled up inside his muddled head as he battled with the climax of fever and pain.

All the while there was Ellen, who became Maura, wee Maura his child. He held her hand as he led the horse down the hay meadow. "Hold on tight to the mane Maura, you won't fall off, that's a good wee girl." The damp cloth, again, cold on his warm brow.

"I'm not Maura, I'm Ellen."

"Oh, I'm sorry, I forgot for a minute." His eyes closed and he dozed again.

"I have to go now John, Seamus is here." Her soft hand touched his cheek. He wanted to beg her not to leave him, but he said nothing.

He was roused by a strong smell of stale whiskey; Seamus was bending over him. "I sent them two home, I'll look after you now. If I'd known you were sick, they wouldn't have got their noses in," his slurred voice caused alarm bells to ring in his brain. "They were very good to me... saved my life," he gasped between painful breaths. "We don't need the likes of them, I'll look after you now," he retorted angrily, throwing himself down on the other bed. Shortly afterwards John heard his loud snores.

The long night wore on, and at times John felt he was losing the battle, as pain accompanied his every breath. As he lay in the semi-darkness he was forced for the first time in his life, to face his own mortality. Regrets for his deeds of the past washed over him like icy ocean waves. "Sara, I'm sorry...ask wee Maura to forgive me," he muttered over, and over.

Seamus bent over him again and shook him by the shoulders. "John, John, wake up. Will you sign here?" John groaned in pain as he heaved him roughly up onto the pillows. "We don't want her claiming anything now do we? Sign here. just in case," he urged, holding the pen between his fingers as he guided his signature onto the paper.

When he awoke in the late morning, his breathing was easier, the sweating had stopped, and he knew the worst was over. But his recovery was slow. He hated his confinement to the house, and for the first time in his life he knew loneliness, as he stared at the empty deserted fields. He was ashamed of his tears; men in his masculine world didn't cry.

Ellen was his only contact with the outside world, he waited patiently for her twice daily visits. She brought him broth, egg-nog and soda bread. He had become totally dependent on her, not only for the food she brought, or for the turf and water she carried in for him, but even more, for the companionship she gave him.

Seamus came only occasionally. Something about Seamus disturbed him; something shadowy, to do with that night when he thought he was dying, but he couldn't remember what it was or why he felt so uneasy in his company.

He started taking short walks outside around the farmyard, but the slightest exertion left him fatigued.

Try as he may, he just couldn't stop himself thinking about Sara and Maura, they seemed to trouble his every waking hour. "Damn them anyway, I don't need them," he shouted repeatedly to the empty kitchen. When the Angelus bell rang out he anxiously looked out the window. 'Where is she anyway? She has never been this late before,' he whispered to himself, as a concerned frown deepened on his face. 'Maybe she thinks I'm well enough to manage on my own,' he debated with himself, as panic began spreading through his whole body. His legs shook when he stood up. 'You can manage on your own John Quinn,' he told himself as he shuffled shakily towards the door. The doctor's, words on his last visit echoed in his ears. "It will take quite a while before you can manage on your own. In addition to the weakness caused by the fever, you are also suffering from depression," he had told him. He stood leaning on the fence for support; his chin resting on his elbows.

The evening sky turned gold, as the sun sank low in the western sky. He looked up and down the lane, but not a soul was in sight. "I will have to try and make it to the well for water before dark. I might have known I couldn't rely on her," he muttered close to tears, tears that angered and shamed him. "Damn you Sara for leaving me in this fix." It was almost two years since he came home and found her gone. He recalled how he had fired the delph around the kitchen in temper when he read her note. There had always been a woman around to look after his needs, first his mother and then Sara. It was his right; their duty, and he had always taken this for granted, until now. Then a strange whimpering sound interrupted his thoughts. At first he thought it was an animal in some kind of pain. He had walked only a few yards into the laneway to investigate, when he saw her sandwiched between the fuchsia bushes, almost hidden from sight. She rocked back and forth in rhythm to the cries of anguish coming from her throat.

"What in the name of heaven is wrong with you?" "I've been waiting for you for ages." She looked up with wild frightened eyes, and sprang to her feet, her clothes were dishevelled, and her torn blouse revealed a bare shoulder. Then she quickly pulled her coat around her, gripping it together with her right hand. He noticed fresh blood around the finger - nails gripping the coat. "Have you been in a fight or something? Try and tell me," he said in a kinder tone.

She shook her head and pointed up the lane, before bolting down the bray towards home. As he watched her disappear, he thought about following her, but then thought better of it. Sitting down on the ditch to rest, he pondered on his next move.

She had pointed up the lane, he knew he must try to find out what happened to her, what had terrified her so much? Walking on slowly up the lane he stopped every few minutes to look and listen, but nothing he saw or heard gave him any clues to explain the state he had found her in. His legs began to shake again. He had to rest. The door of Seamus's cottage was half open. Maybe Seamus could throw some light on the mystery and he could rest at the same time.

Pushing the door open he went in, and stood for a few seconds adjusting his eyes to the gloomy interior. Then he saw him as he bent over a bowl of water at the table, his braces hanging loose over his knees. Unaware of John's presence he continued to bathe his face, while all around him the room looked a shambles, chairs were overturned, and broken delph littered the floor. Suddenly realising he was not alone he looked up, it was then that John saw the angry red scratch running the full length of his face. The expression in his eyes went from fear to guilt. "I..., I scratched myself shaving,," he said with a nervous laugh. Suddenly John was gripped by an awful fear, as the truth slowly dawned on him.

"I was just out for a stroll, tired of the four walls. I must get back, the fire will be out," he said trying to sound casual.

John didn't remember how he got back down the lane to the house. He sat in the kitchen, with the door bolted, while a thousand mocking, taunting, demons ran amock in his head, and the haunted terrified face of Ellen Murphy came looming up in front of his eyes.

He could barely allow himself to think about Maura; Seamus had violated his own child, and he had called them damned liars when they tried to tell him.

He was not sure how much time had passed, so absorbed was he in his mental torment. He was suddenly aware that darkness had fallen. He lit the lamp and put turf on the fire hoping that the warmth would stop the shivering of his limbs. Suddenly, he was seized by a great anger such as he had never known before, his whole being cried out for revenge.

The gun was hidden under the bed. Getting down on his knees, and using a curtain pole he eased it out far enough to grab hold of it. It was then his eye caught sight of his fountain pen, but why was it here? He had always kept it in the kitchen drawer. Then memory began to return... "sign here. You don't want her coming back to claim anything."

"So you thought I was going to die, and you would be the new owner. Damn you to hell, I'll show you who will die first," he shouted as he frantically pulled open drawers and cupboards in his search for cartridges.
Finally forced to give up the search in defeat, he slumped exhausted into the chair putting the empty gun on his lap.

Chapter 4

To Start Anew

The road from Ballyneely station to the rectory was all-uphill. John Quinn sat down periodically along the side of the road to rest. His health had never recovered from the illness of a year ago, he became breathless on the least exertion. He knew that his race was nearly run, time was not on his side, it was now or never. With a sigh of relief he reached the stone pillars heralding the entrance to the avenue.

In the distance he saw a pony and trap coming towards him, he dived for cover behind the pillar, as the trap passed between the gateway he peered out. Sara was holding the reins, he didn't recognise the elderly woman with her.

Sitting down he rested his head against the pillar trying to collect his thoughts. It was a shock seeing her again after all this time, he would have to wait now until she came back. This was a setback, he wanted to get it over with as quickly as possible. As he watched the autumn leaves swirling around in the wind his thoughts once again returned for the umpteenth time to the awful events of the last year, events that changed him into a humble quivering wreck filled with deep regret and shame, a shame that tortured his very soul.

How would he face Sara? He didn't expect forgiveness, but he had to try and explain.

His mind went back to the night when he sat with the empty gun on his lap. An hour or more had passed before he heard the latch being lifted.

Seamus walked in and sat down as usual, he didn't notice the gun at first. John was filled with a rage that consumed him totally, he wanted revenge like he never wanted anything before. Looking back he was in no doubt that had he found the cartridges he would have blown his brains out and then turned the gun on himself. They sat in silence for a minute or so, Seamus spoke first.

"Cleaning the gun?" he said casually.

"I'm cleaning it for you... for you, you evil bastard." John sprang to his feet and pushed the barrel into his temple.

"Have you gone mad, it's me, John. The fever must have affected your brain, put the gun away."

"My brain has never been clearer. You attacked that wee girl earlier, you raped her like you raped my daughter, you evil spawn of the devil." He pushed the gun harder into his temple as he spoke.

"Take it easy, you got it wrong," he stammered with

fear in his voice.

"Don't try and lie to me, it won't wash any more you swine. They told me it was you, I didn't believe them, I didn't, believe my own wife and daughter. Running around with every Tom, Dick and Harry you said, and I believed you, to my sorrow and shame I believed you." He again pushed the gun into his flesh.

"Take it easy John," his quivering voice was barely audible. "You got it wrong, I..."

"Shut up, stop attempting to lie any more, I saw the wee girl, clothes torn and terrified. Then I went in search of you, one look was all I needed. So don't even try to lie to me again." He looked down into Seamus's face, the eyes staring back were filled with terror, he knew the game was up. "I suppose you have got the Will you forced me to sign safely tucked away, thought I was dying, too far gone to notice. Man you thought of everything, didn't you." He pushed his head further to the side with the gun as he spoke. "Have you any last words before I blow your evil brains out?"

"Don't do it John, give me a chance. I'll make it up to you. It was easy for you. You had a wife. I never had a woman..., you know what I mean," he faltered.

"Let me see if I've got this right, you never had a woman so you decided to prey on young innocent girls...to rape wee girls. If this is your only defence then God, have mercy on your evil soul. Get down on your knees, down I said." He shoved the gun harder into his flesh.

"No please John I'll go away, anything you want, but don't shoot," he began to cry out in terror.

"Say your prayers."

"Our.. Father..." he began to mumble.

"Our Seamus destined for the religious life if only he were stronger. That's what your mother always said, she must have been rolling in her grave all these years." He stared down at his bent head and wished again that he had a cartridge, just one would do it.

"Get up for God's sake." He watched him rise shakily to his feet. "Sit back in the chair," he barked. "I have decided to let you live, you are not worth the powder that would blow your brains out anyway." He watched the colour come back to his face, though he was still shaking uncontrollably. "I am giving you twelve hours to get out, away from here as far away as you can get. If you have any ideas about doing me in, forget it. I left a letter with the Sergeant to be opened if I should mysteriously disappear. If you are not gone by the deadline, you get no second chance," he yelled into his ear. "I won't be short of help in the neighbourhood in getting rid of your remains if you don't heed my warning," he repeated, escorting him to the door at gun point.

Seamus Quinn took the warning and disappeared. From a back window John watched him leave in Molly's pony and trap.

As the days and weeks passed slowly, he spent the time in

solitude trying to come to terms with all that had happened. He felt humble and betrayed, but most of all he hated himself. These emotions were totally new to him, always so sure he was right, always master of his own destiny. But now he had to face the fact that he had been an arrogant bully, and for his sins he had lost everything. In isolation and with his health fading, he had to make difficult heartrending decisions.

Wee Ellen Murphy had not visited him since that awful day when he found her in the hedge. He had seen her occasionally passing on her way to school, but gone was the happy smile, and carefree air of childhood; it had all been stolen from her. He needed to talk to her Mother, he owed her an explanation of some sort. He must reassure her that Seamus would not be back.

He waited for his chance to talk to her alone, he had rightly guessed that she would come to the well about ten, in the morning for water. When she had filled her buckets he approached her. At first she looked like she was about to take flight, her eyes darted wildly around, and her face looked troubled. John swallowed hard before he spoke. "I need to talk to you Grace," he began in a quiet gentle voice. "Did Ellen tell you anything, about him?" he asked nodding back up the lane. Grace put the buckets down, again a look of fear and panic crossed her face before she answered. "Not a word about it must ever be mentioned to a living soul. Her father doesn't even know, if he had he would probably have been hung for murder by now."

John nodded in understanding. As he told her about the events following his grim discovery, she just shook her head. Her knees shaking out of control, she sat down on the ditch to regain her composure.

"I'm glad you didn't find the cartridges, he isn't worth hanging for.

About Sara, do you know where she is?"
He shook his head.

"I know. And if you promise to go and make your peace with her, I'll tell you where she is. Just tell her what you told me," she added. He remained silent for a moment, then he spoke again.

"How do you know where she is?" he asked.

"That doesn't matter, I just know." He made patterns in the dust of the lane with his walking stick before saying anything.

"Tell me where she is? I doubt if she will want to see me and who could blame her, but I'll try."

He was numb with the cold as he pulled himself up from where he was sitting at the rectory gates, and as the trap hadn't returned, he decided that he couldn't sit in the cold any longer. He would go on up to the rectory and wait, the yard was deserted. He noticed smoke coming from the kitchen chimney. "At least someone is at home," he whispered in relief. Taking a deep breath he knocked on the kitchen door. Eventually after a lot of shuffling the door creaked open. Molly Sheehey stood there, propping herself up with the aid of a stick.

He barely recognised her. When he last saw her in his courting days she was a strong agile woman. She stared at him without recognition. Clearing his throat he said, "I've come to see Sara, it's important" he added. He watched her face change and her eyes harden as recognition came to her.

"She isn't here, and anyhow she won't want to see you that's for sure," her voice sounded hostile.

"I know that she won't be overjoyed to see me, but I just need to talk to her, it's very important. Can I come in and wait please? I don't mean her any harm." She saw his frail frame shake with the cold, and she reluctantly stepped aside.

"I suppose I can let you in for a few minutes to get warm, but you better be gone before she gets back," she warned.

As he followed her slow lumbering frame inside, he caught sight of the small figure peeping from behind her skirt. The blue eyes, the brown curls; he thought he was looking at Maura as she was all those years ago. He could feel the hair standing up on the back of his neck as he watched her. He sat down at the big table still watching the little figure peering at him from behind a chair.

"This is the little soul that you abandoned, your granddaughter," she said as she watched him staring at the child.

"I know what you think of me Molly. But I am no

threat to any of you. I'm not the man I was, I have learned a bitter lesson or two since Sara left. I want to try to make my peace with her while there is still time."

Looking at him more closely she was again shocked at his gaunt face, the grey pallor, and his obvious frailty.

"Would you like a cup of tea?" He nodded.

He watched as she made the tea and sliced the home made bread without getting to her feet. As if reading his thoughts she commented.

"I'm all right from the waist up, but the legs have gone. Sara came just in time, if she hadn't come when she did, I would have been in the workhouse by now. You're loss was my gain." He drank the hot sweet tea, and ate the bread as he listened to Molly.

"Sara is the most courageous woman I have ever known. "God only knows she has an awful burden, a helpless child, an old woman, a cripple, and a drunk all in her care. She needs you like a hole in the head, and just when things were beginning to look brighter for us. Aye, she needs you like a hole in the head," she repeated. Then lifting Mary Kate onto her knee she told him about Sara's courage and their recent struggle to survive.

Chapter 5

Sarah's Struggle

Sara pulled the scarf over her ears, then slinging the bundle of sticks over her shoulder she struggled up from the shore, bent under their weight. The storm had brought in the much, needed firewood on the tide. The last few weeks had been the greatest test of her entire life, a desperate struggle to survive. Her money had all gone and they were down to the last quarter bag of flour. Sitting down to rest, she stared out at the rough Atlantic ocean. A liner lay anchored in the shelter of the bay.

Her thoughts went back to Maura and her description of the storm on her long voyage to America. The letter she sent was the only thing that gave her the courage to struggle on.

In the letter she had promised to send money as soon as she got paid. "We will hold out until then," she said aloud to herself through gritted teeth.

In the kitchen she laid down the sticks and began to light a fire.

Molly and Mary Kate stayed in bed for most of the day to try and keep warm. When the fire was finally alight she put her scarf back on to go in search of milk.

She sighed at the thought of going back to the Malloney's for milk without money to pay for it.

She was still burning with the humiliation she felt when she tried to get goods on credit in Ballyneely. One by one they shook their heads when she told them who it was for.

"He owes too much already," they said.

But pride was a small price when Mary Kate needed milk.

Mary Maloney filled her jug with milk. If it had been her husband he wouldn't have been so generous, he had only half filled it yesterday.

"I'll pay you as soon as I can," Sara said.

"Don't worry at all about it, sure there will be milk galore when we are all dead. Do you need potatoes?" she asked.

"Thank you Mary, may God bless you for your goodness," Sara said humbled by her neighbour's kindness. Walking back she gave thanks to God, for giving them the means to survive for today at least.

"Is that you Sara, Molly called?"

"Aye it's me, you can get up now if you like, I've got the milk," she called back to her.

Mary Kate drank the milk greedily, Molly watched her in silence.

"One of the sycamore trees along the avenue blew

down last night, if I had help to cut it up we would have plenty of firewood, Sara remarked.

Molly made no reply, she was lost in her own thoughts of hopelessness. James Thompson had never gone away for so long before. Was he long dead in some ditch, or alley-way, she wondered? "How long has it been since he left, do you remember Sara?" she asked.

"It's over three months anyway, Sara sighed. "We have to face it he isn't coming back Molly, he would have written or something before now, we will have to survive somehow on our own.

"Would it not have been better if you had left that wee soul in the convent? At least she would have been fed."

"No, shut your stupid mouth and mind your own business. Why the hell do you think I am suffering all this? I could still be at home. I'm doing it for Mary Kate," she screamed back at her.

Molly was so shocked by the anger of her outburst that she burst into tears, her shoulders shaking with sobs. In spite of his drinking Molly was fond of James Thompson, he had been good to her in his own way. She refused to believe that he had deliberately disappeared like Sara was maintaining. But hope of his return was fading with every day that passed. Mary Kate began to whimper, as she watched their angry faces closely. Sara picked her up and gave her a reassuring cuddle. Carrying her over to Molly she put her free arm around her heaving shoulders.

"I know it's hard for you too. I'm sorry I shouted at you."

"No, I'm the one who shouldn't have said what I did, sure I love her nearly as much as you."

"We won't fight any more between ourselves, we need one another if we are to survive to see better times." Molly nodded in agreement wiping her tears away with the tail of her apron.

Sara finally reached the back door with her heavy burden. The daily search for firewood was exhausting. She had to walk further and further afield each day. Closing the door she threw them on the floor.

"Sara, a letter came, Henry brought it up. It's from America," Molly greeted her excitedly.

Quickly cleaning her hands on her coat Sara tore open the letter. She counted out twenty crisp dollars. While reading Maura's letter, tears of relief ran unchecked down her face.

"I must get down to Ballyneely before dark if we are to get a good supper tonight," she said with a broad smile.

"I told Henry to catch the pony, just in case," Molly added cheerfully.

Turf for the fire had to be her first priority. The pony pulled up outside the turf-man's cottage.

"If it's good hard well saved turf you're wanting Pat's your man. And he has two strapping sons. They would soon make short work of that tree," Henry advised before she left.

Telling Pat about Henry's recommendation of him, she got the promise of a cart load before dark, and his sons said they would come in the morning to cut up the tree in the drive.

As she was about to get back into the trap he said, "He is not renowned in these parts as much of a payer..... Thompson, I mean."

"I am doing the paying, the money will be waiting for you."

"I had to make sure."

"I know you did," Sara said, getting back into the trap.

The drawing room fire blazed and crackled merrily, scenting the air with wood and turf. Sara looked around the room with its lovely old furnishings. She had spent weeks getting it back into shape. At first sight she thought it was beyond redemption, but her hard work had paid off.

The dry and sunny late summer had made it a lot easier, she had taken everything she could outside for airing and cleaning. The long discarded drapes she found in the attic were a big improvement, on the mouldy moth eaten ones that she had to throw out. She had always loved this room, even all those years ago as a maid, cleaning it was her favourite job. But what was the point now, no one even sat in it. Going back to the kitchen she had an idea.

"Molly we are going to sit in the drawing room

tonight."

"But what if he comes back?"

"So what if he does, we might as well have a wee bit of comfort."

"You're right, I think we have earned it," Molly said getting stiffly to her feet.

Two weeks later Sara prepared the drawing room for the evening as usual, she piled wood and turf on the fire, before going over to the window to look out at the snow storm that was rapidly turning into a blizzard.

A sound from the doorway startled her. She swung around. He stood in the door, wet snow dripping from his long grey overcoat. Her mouth opened wide in astonishment.

"My God, we thought you were dead, long dead," she added.

"On the law of averages I should be dead. Had a bad accident in Dublin, I was unconscious for a long time. And for once I wasn't drunk when it happened. A runaway horse and cart they told me."

She noticed a long scar on his forehead, and he looked much thinner.

"Could you not have sent us word? Things were desperate here."

"I tried to but that story will keep. I'm sorry about all the hardships you had. Molly just told me all about it in the kitchen a few minutes ago."

He looked around the room as if seeing it for the first

time. "You have done an amazing job here, I thought this room was beyond repair."

He sat down in the armchair by the fire, holding his hands close to the flames.

"I haven't sat in this room since she died. We spent many happy hours in here. Oh, what's the use, I can't bring her back," he added staring into the flames.

"You know I expected the place to be empty, instead I find all this" he said, waving his hand around the room.

"I'll get you some tea and a bite to eat. Do you want it in here by the fire?" she asked.

"That would be grand, thanks," he added, taking off his top coat. A few minutes later she brought the food in on a tray and put it down on a side table.

"I have a proposition to put to you. It can wait until tomorrow, I'm too tired now. Thanks again," he said before she closed the door. Sara stood with her back to the closed door.

'What was his proposal going to be about?' she wondered. And they were just about to make themselves comfortable in the drawing room for the evening, as always.

'Was it off with the new, and on with the old again?' she wondered, as she went back to the kitchen with a heavy heart; back to sit on the hard wooden chairs. 'And just as we were beginning to take for granted the comfort of the drawing room in the evenings,' she thought with a pang of regret.

The old familiar smell of stale alcohol greeted Sara's nostrils when she brought his breakfast. He barely grunted in response to her morning greeting, she put down the tray and left the room with a heavy heart.

The snow had stopped by the afternoon and, the sun came out. Wrapping Mary Kate up warmly Sara said. "I'm taking you out for a wee walk to see your first snow."

Outside Sara watched her playing in the snow, falling down, and rolled around with squeals of delight. 'If only your mother could see you now,' she smiled with pleasure. She loved these special moments spent with Mary Kate. She was delighted with how well she had grown and thrived in the past year.

Then he suddenly appeared around the corner.

"I see she is enjoying the snow. She is growing fast."

"Aye, she is Mr. Thompson, in spite of near starvation a while back, she's still thriving."

"I'm sorry you all had to suffer like that," he looked away guiltily.

"I was the one who wanted to come," Sara said briskly.

"You offered to work without pay, but not without food. To prevent this happening again I must talk to you, when you have time, I'll be up in the study."

He crunched his way back through the snow, leaving Sara to wonder about what he was up to.

Later that evening she knocked on the study door.

He was seated in the leather chair, a whiskey bottle on the table beside him.

"Sit down, I've been waiting for you."

She sat on the chair opposite him and, waited.

"I'm in a lot of debt," he began. "My money is all gone, long gone. That is why I went to Dublin. I have an elderly maiden aunt living there. Then I had the accident, but we won't go into that now." I asked her for help, financial help. We came to a sort of agreement, and this is where you come in." I was going to sell the place, and go to Canada or somewhere.

He gave her a long searching look before continuing.

"She agreed to pay my debts if she could have a home here with us. Aunt Jean is an old woman, she would need a bit of looking after.Could you manage do you think? I know it's a lot to ask; another burden on an overloaded back. If you refuse I won't blame you. Just think it over and let me know," he added lamely.

Sara sat staring into the fire when he had finished talking. Part of her wanted to scream, 'no, I have too much on my plate already, what the hell do you think I am?' Instead she asked. "What kind of a woman is this aunt of yours?"

"She is a kind woman, and I should know for she reared me." He took a gulp of the whiskey before going on. "My father was killed in a hunting accident, and my mother died of consumption shortly after, leaving me an orphan. Aunt Jean brought me up," he concluded.

"Very well then I'll do my best for her."

Molly reacted angrily, when Sara told her the news. "You must be out of your mind to agree to it. You have no idea what it will be like. She will expect to be waited on hand and foot. I can just imagine it, bells clanging at all hours of the day and night. I have memories of that one from old, and I for one don't want to see her inside this house," she retorted angrily.

"I know it won't be easy. But at least she might keep us fed," Sara said, trying not to think of Molly's dooms day scenario.

There was little time to think much about the consequences of her decision. A room had to be prepared and aired for the new arrival. She spent her evenings patching bed linen and repairing holes in the curtains.

"That is six patches I have put on this sheet," Sara said, putting the sheet down with a sigh.

"This wee wain should be in her bed, she is more important than sewing sheets for that old tarter. Let her go and buy sheets for herself." Mary Kate had fallen asleep on Molly's lap. Sara picked up the sleeping infant without comment.

"You be sure and tell her that I'm not fit to cook fancy dishes anymore." Pretending not to hear her, Sara carried the child to bed. Molly was grating on her nerves, she made it obvious that she didn't want any intrusions into her domain. She sat in the old rocking chair watching the baby as she slept in her cot. The faint, smell of lavender still scented the air. "Why am I willing to work my fingers to the bone for nothing?" she asked herself. With Maura's monthly money I could rent a wee cottage somewhere and keep poultry, it would be a damned sight easier than trying to keep this big, ramshackle, place with its hopeless and helpless inhabitants. It was as if the house had some kind of hold on her, and she was its willing slave.

Getting up from the chair she left the sanctuary of the nursery and went back downstairs to help Molly into bed; her last duty of a long weary day.

As she helped Molly undress a feeling of deep compassion came over her, she could suddenly understand how she could feel threatened and vulnerable about the new situation.

"Molly, listen to me, I won't desert you no matter what. If this old aunt of his turns out to be as bad as you fear we will go, just remember I will always look after you somehow," she said.

Molly's sad eyes met Sara's. "May God bless you Sara, I am truly blessed in having a friend like you." She squeezed Sara's hand as a tear ran down her cheek.

At the sound of the approaching train Sara got out of the trap and stood by the pony's head. This was the moment she had dreaded for the past month. Would Molly's warning come true, would this old woman turn their world upside down?

She watched them alight from the train, Mr. Thompson holding her arm protectively as they approached her

"This is my aunt, Jean Thompson," he said as they came up close to her.

"You must be Sara, I have heard so much about you from my nephew here," she said with a warm smile. The handshake was firm and her eyes were kind. Sara knew immediately that she was going to like Jean Thompson.

The pony made slow progress up the hill with the heavy load of passengers and luggage. At last the gates to the driveway came into view and the pony quickened his step. Very little conversation passed between them since they left the station. Sara drove the trap up to the front door.

"Your room is ready, you can go straight to bed if you wish," Sara said with a smile, as she helped her out of the trap.

"Thank you dear, I'll be as little trouble to you as I can. I can still do most things for myself," she concluded. Sara breathed a sigh of relief, she knew that she would get along fine with this frail old lady with her kindly smile.

Later in the kitchen she gave Molly the good news. But to her astonishment Molly was as hostile as before about the new arrival.

"You are a fool Sara Quinn if you fall for that. Just you wait until she has been here a while."

"I'm a fairly good judge of character, she has a kind face and I'm sure she will give us no trouble. She even said she will eat her meals with us in the kitchen here."

"Be damned to that, we don't need an old tarter like that spying on us. I'd carry the food to her on all fours to keep her nose out of my kitchen."

"Just wait until you meet her Molly before you make judgements."

When Jean Thompson made her first appearance in the kitchen the following day Molly's resentment of her was made obvious.

"I'm sorry to hear about your rheumatism, it must be painful, Miss Thompson said in a sympathetic tone.

"I manage, I can still cook as well as ever, and that is without getting paid a penny for it," she said coldly, while glowering at her sarcastically.

"I'm sorry that things have been so bad for you. I know what a mess he has made of everything."
Molly was not impressed by her kind words, she continued to stare at the newcomer with hostility, much to Sara's annoyance.

Sara carried Mary Kate the last few yards up the steep hill from the shore. They had spent a happy hour on the beach. It was the first sunny day in a long time, and Sara decided to take a little of her scarce time to get Mary Kate out in the fresh air. At the top of the hill she was startled to see Jean Thompson. She was staring out to sea lost in thought.

"Are you all right?" Sara asked. She blinked for a few seconds before answering.

"I'm fine. Just remembering the past and what might have been," she sighed.

"I spent my summers here as a young girl, long before your time. As you know Reverend Thompson was my older brother. It was so nice to get away from Dublin and come here to, all this freedom, with its wild and beautiful landscape. I didn't like my sister-in-law much, so I stayed out of her way. I spent most of my time rambling around the hills and shores. I fell in love here one summer. I was nineteen then." She stroked Mary Kate's curly head before she spoke again. "He was drowned just beyond those rocks. I remember it as though it happened yesterday."

"I'm sorry it must have been awful for you," Sara said breaking the silence.

"It seemed like my world had come to an end," she continued. "He was a local fisherman, I can just see him now, tall with a mop of black curly hair. Of course being a fisherman and Catholic he was deemed to be totally unsuitable as a partner for me," she said coldly. "His family felt just as hostile about it so we planned to elope to America." She let out a long sigh of regret as she stood up to go. "Sara would you take me over to Ballyneely graveyard in the trap someday? I would like to visit his grave, it might help me to bury some of the ghosts from the past."

"I will surely. Anytime you want," Sara said as they began walking in silence through the gate of the walled garden towards the house. "I will always be willing to look after the little one for you, in fact it would give me the greatest pleasure. You are lucky to have her," she added wistfully, reaching down and taking Mary Kate by the hand.

"Thank you, but it's a bit awkward, it's Molly, you see, she usually keeps an eye on her for me."

"I understand perfectly," Jean broke in. "Poor Molly would feel she was really being pushed to one side, I know she already feels threatened by my arrival. I'll just have to keep trying to convince her that I mean her no harm. I will go around to the side entrance, don't want to cause any more jealousy, eh," she said before disappearing around the corner of the house.

Sara picked Mary Kate up in her arms, and watched as she disappeared around the corner of the house. Her thoughts were on the curley haired, fisherman, and the romance of old Jean's youth. She wanted to hear more about her past. She found her fascinating, and she was already very fond of her. But, she knew that she must keep these thoughts a secret from Molly's jealous ears.

The following week Jean was laid low with a fever which developed into bronchitis. The doctor was called. He gave them very little hope of her recovering. "Her age and frailty is against her," he told Sara shaking his head. "Just keep her propped up in bed, and give her plenty of fluids. It's in God's hands now," he added. Sara nursed her around the clock, sometimes almost asleep on her feet. Mr. Thompson came to see her every day, he was very upset, and usually consoled himself with the whiskey bottle.

"I hate seeing her like this, she is all I have left," he told Sara in a slurred voice." I don't know what we would do without you Sara. "If there is a God, then he sent you here."

"I'm just doing what I can for her, I've grown very fond of your Aunt in the short while I have known her. I just hope and pray that she is spared for another while," Sara said, as she mopped her brow with a cold flannel.

Two weeks later Jean Thompson was well enough to sit out in the armchair at the side of her bed. Although still weak, she was cheerful.

"I'm going to live to fight another day," she told Sara as she helped her out of bed. "Don't forget to bring Mary Kate up to see me, when you get time. I look forward to seeing her, she lifts my spirits no end. She is such a lovely little thing, and clever with it," she beamed.

"I'll take her up when Molly goes for her afternoon rest," Sara reassured her.

It was autumn before Jean was well enough to make the

journey to the grave. They waited for a dry bright day before setting off in the pony and trap.

"Tell Molly we are going to the shops. I would rather she didn't know about the grave." Jean said.
Sara was a little baffled by her need for secrecy.

Before reaching the driveway gates Sara saw a shadow disappear behind one of the pillars. She looked around her as she drove through but although she saw nothing, still she had a feeling they were being watched. As the trap drew level with Henry's cottage, he hurried out the door.

"Wait a minute Sara, the postman left a letter for you this morning," he said, handing her a white envelope.

"It's from Maura. Thank God," she said with a sigh of relief.

"Go on, pull the trap in and read it, I'm in no hurry," Jean urged.

While the pony grazed by the roadside, Sara read Maura's letter to Jean.

Chapter 6

New York 1925

The decks were filled with passengers, as the ship was about to dock. Maura and Hannah stood side by side on the upper deck. They silently watched the quay come closer and closer.

Maura felt fearful at what might lie ahead, and she was suddenly reluctant to leave the safety of the ship.

"I wonder if Aunt Mary is down there somewhere waiting for us?" Hannah's voice broke into her thoughts.

"What on earth will she think, when she finds that she has a penniless stranger to contend with?"

"She will be only too pleased to help," Hannah said reassuringly.

Aunt Mary was a large cheerful woman with a heart to match her bulk. She welcomed Maura with open arms.

"Any friend of Hannah's is a friend of mine," she said warmly, giving Maura a big motherly kiss on the cheek. "Mind you the place is a bit cramped, but we will all get along just fine. Don't look so worried. Cheer up. You are in America. Who knows you might even make your fortune," she added with a loud infectious laugh.

Maura soon began to relax in the company of this big cheery happy family. They were loud, and constantly bickered amongst themselves, but they were always kind and full of fun.

New York came as a great culture shock to the raw newcomers with its noisy traffic, and mass of hustling rushing people. They were afraid to venture far without the guidance of one or two of Aunt Mary's street, wise children. They spent a happy carefree week exploring their strange new surroundings, neither daring to stray far from their young escorts.

Maura felt uneasy about her lack of money, she knew that she must find work soon. She couldn't impose on these kind people any longer. She noticed an employment office in passing one day.

The window had a large sign written in large bold print.

WANTED, DOMESTIC SERVANTS, MAIDS , NANNIES, ETC.

Maura sat in the outer office clutching her bag containing her references nervously. One from the Parish priest, the other from the convent. She could hear a man's loud angry voice coming from the interview room.

"You promised you would have someone else for me today. I told you how urgent it is.

"It is not easy to find someone suitable to look after a

young infant Mr Jefferson," a woman's voice answered. "And anyway I thought the girl I found for you three weeks ago was very suitable" she continued.

"Damn it woman, what good is that, she walked out without even a week's notice," he bellowed back at her.

"She had good reason for walking out as far as I could gather. You would need to do something about that house-keeper of yours if you want to keep staff," her sharp raised voice echoed through the closed door.

"I am paying you to find suitable staff not to make judgements about my house keeper," he shouted back.

The door burst open, a tall angry looking man filled the door space. A middle aged woman followed hard on his heels. He looked at Maura sitting nervously on the edge of her seat.

"Have you any experience at looking after infants? he asked abruptly.

Maura nodded.

"Where?"

"In a, er..., convent," she stammered.

"Have you any references?"

She fumbled in her bag and handed him the two references. He read them quickly before looking back at her.

"You have got yourself a job, that is if you want it. I will pay you twenty dollars a month. My son is five months old," he added before Maura had a chance to answer him.

"This is highly irregular, Mr. Jefferson," the woman

said angrily.

"You will get your damned money, even though you didn't earn it." She glared back at him red faced with anger.

He followed her back into the inner office.

Alone Maura felt stunned. She needed more time to think, should she accept this big angry mans job offer or not. Twenty dollars a month was a lot of money, and she needed the work.

When he reappeared a few minutes later she had decided to accept his offer.

Hannah and her family were concerned about Maura's quick decision to accept the job.

"God knows what kind of a man he is. Where is this job?" Aunt Mary asked anxiously.

"I forgot to ask for his address."

"Well young woman you are not leaving here until we at least know where you are going to. Is he waiting for you outside?" she asked. Maura nodded, feeling very foolish.

"Come on we will get a look at this employer of yours, and find out where he is taking you."

He sat in the back seat of the motor car tapping a cigarette on a silver case impatiently. The chauffeur stared straight ahead. Tapping on the window Mary asked him for his address. Without answering he reached into his jacket pocket and produced a card. Mary thanked him before leaving.

"He's an ill mannered snob if you ask me," she said to Maura when they were out of earshot.

"Jefferson Shipping Company," she read from the card. "Wealthy, no doubt but if they don't treat you right, you come straight back here," she ordered.

They all kissed her goodbye on the doorstep. When it came to saying goodbye to Hannah, Maura couldn't stop the tears.

"I can never thank you enough, you are the best friend anyone could ever wish for. I hope someday I will be able to repay you," she added, before getting into the motor car. They waved until the car was out of sight.

Mr. Jefferson remained silent for most of the journey. Maura sat on the opposite seat, glancing at him occasionally when he wasn't looking. He lit one cigarette after the other, blinking nervously as he stared out of the window.

"I will introduce you to the housekeeper when we get there, she will show you the ropes. I have an urgent appointment to attend to" he added. "My wife is in poor health at the moment," he continued, "she is staying with her mother".

"I'm sorry to hear that. I hope she will soon get better."

He nodded, and lit another cigarette. The motor car drove through a wide gateway.

Rounding the curve of the driveway she caught her first sight of the house. She stared in amazement at the sheer size of it, wide sweeping steps led up to the porch, with a line of large gothic pillars running the full length of it. Maura stood in the large hall and admired the beauty and luxury that surrounded her. The long graceful staircase, the crystal chandeliers, the rich red carpets, the paintings and the beautiful ornaments almost took her breath away.

"This is Miss Hanley, my housekeeper," Mr. Jefferson's voice made her jump, so engrossed was she in her surroundings.

Turning around she saw a middle-aged woman with greying hair in a neat bun. Her thin lips smiled, but her eyes were cold. Maura shuddered, she had a sense of foreboding about this woman that spelt a bad omen.

"Pleased to meet you Miss er..."

"Quinn, Maura Quinn," Mr Jefferson filled in for her.

"Well then Maura I'll show what to do, Mr. Jefferson has to be on his way," she said smiling up at her employer.

As soon as he went out the door the smile left her face. "Follow me, I'll show you the nursery."

Maura followed her up two flights of stairs. Before ascending the third flight she could hear the baby's cries. Opening a door at the far end of the corridor she turned to Maura.

"This is the nursery, you sleep in here beside the infant. I will get someone to show you where the kitchen is presently," she continued, raising her voice above the baby's yells. "Use the back stairs, the front stairs are for use by myself and the family only. "For goodness sake try and shut him up," she shouted at Maura. Picking up the baby Maura tried to comfort him, rocking him to and fro in her arms until his crying gradually ceased.

"Thank heaven, for that, I will send the maid up to show you where the kitchen is. You will eat your meals in here," she continued. "You do not leave the nursery, apart from when you go to the kitchen to collect his feeds."
Maura could feel a shiver going down her spine; She sensed trouble ahead in the person of Ethel Hanley.
She closed the nursery door leaving her alone with her charge. Maura had to fight the feeling of panic that suddenly welled up in her throat. She was now solely responsible for this small being, 'what do I really know about babies?' she asked herself out loud, "and there is no one to help." As she fought with her fear she heard a welcome knock on the door.

"Come in," she called. A dark haired girl came in dressed in a black frock, with a white apron and mop cap.

"My name Maria, I come from Italy. Speak only little English," she said with a broad grin.

"Can you show me where the kitchen is?" Maura asked. "You follow, I show you." As they went down the stairs Maria stopped suddenly. Putting a finger to her lips she listened for a few seconds before speaking.

"Miss Hanley she bad woman, she bitch, make bad for everybody," she warned. The cook was also Italian and spoke even less English than Maria.

Maura had to communicate with sign language as best she could. Through trial and error she learned to cope with looking after the baby. He cried less, and less as she became more confident about handling him.

The days passed slowly, apart from Maria and the cook she had no other adult company.

A long lonely month passed. She had not seen her employer since the day of her arrival, neither did she see the child's mother. No wonder Maria said, "poor bambino," every time she looked at him. He might as well have been an orphan for all the interest his parents showed in him Maura thought.

Miss Hanley came occasionally to check up on her, and always found something to criticise her for. Maura came to dread her visits. The words of the woman at the employment office came back to her when Maria came to tell her tearfully that she was leaving. "Hanley bad woman, bitch, you be careful," was all Maura could make out as she rambled on in Italian. She spat on the floor to show her hatred of the housekeeper, then she kissed Maura on the cheek and was gone. Maria's departure came as another blow to her flagging spirits, leaving her more lonely and isolated than ever. She wrote endless letters to her mother, it made her feel close to her, even though she had no money left to post them.

Thoughts of home were very much at the forefront of her mind. It was strange that the recent past seemed to be blocked out. In memory she was always a child, safe and secure and loved. She saw herself running down the lane to school, roaming the hills and dales with her school friends in the summer, sitting on her father's knee on winter nights while he told her stories. It was as if she had wiped out her adult life, blocking out the events that caused her to hate her father. Her dreams always took her back home, they always seemed so real, she could hear the lark's song on a still evening, smell the turf smoke, and see her mother always smiling as she welcomed her home. Dreaming was an escape from the frightening loneliness of the present.

Accidentally finding the library gave her sagging spirits a lift, she often read until the wee hours. She thanked God for the written word, and the library's irresistible treasures.

Heavy footsteps sounded in the corridor, suddenly the nursery door was flung open. His sheer bulk filled the doorway. Maura stared at him in astonishment.

"Hello there, I'm Andrew, Andrew Jefferson he boomed. I'm this little fellow's uncle." In a couple of strides he was over to where Maura was seated with the baby on her lap.

"You have grown since I last saw you, young David," he said holding out his arms. "May I?" She stood up and handed him the child, who took one look at him, opened his mouth and let out a high pitched scream. "It seems I will have to hand him back, he doesn't seem to like me much," he said handing him back to Maura. "I'm sorry I forgot to ask your name."

"It's Maura Quinn."

"Pretty name, and pretty girl too."

Maura could feel her face blush as he sat down on the chair opposite her.

"How long have you been here?"

"Almost six weeks, but it seems longer," she said. His piercing blue eyes looking into hers made her feel self-conscious.

"Do I detect an Irish lilt?" Maura nodded.

"Well, how do you like America? Is it the brave new world you had hoped for?" he continued.

"I don't know yet, I have seen very little of it."

"We will have to change that, you must see some of the sights of New York. What do you do on your days off?" he asked.

"I haven't had any days off yet. I have been here in the nursery all the time since I arrived," she said.

"What, not even one day off in six weeks. Good God what the hell is he playing at!"
He got up from the chair and began pacing up and down the floor.

"I haven't seen Mr. Jefferson, or the baby's mother since I came." He swung around to face her again.

"I can't believe what I am hearing. You mean to tell me that you have been here on your own, around the clock for six weeks without a break?"

He sat down again in the chair with his head in his hands. Maura watched him in silence, his long fingers moving through his crisp blonde hair. Finally he looked up at her again.

"Maura, will you leave this with me. If you agree to stay, I will see that you get at least one day a week off. I'm sorry about all this," he added with a sigh. "Have you been out with him in the fresh air?" he asked as he reached over and touched the baby's hand.

"Only once, he is getting a bit heavy to carry far. And anyway Miss Hanley says I am not allowed to take him out of the nursery," Maura replied.

"To hell with that old witch," he bellowed angrily. I will never know why my mother didn't get rid of her years ago. Take no notice of her, wheel him out in the fresh air. It will do you both good." he added.

"Thank you Mr. Jefferson, I would like that, but I don't think he has a baby carriage."

"Just leave it with me, I will have transport for young David by morning. Oh, and by the way has that brother of mine paid you yet?" he asked.

Maura shook her head. "Not yet."

He reached into his inside jacket pocket, and put some notes down on the table before walking to the door.

He stood in the doorway for a few seconds, then changed his mind and went back to where they were sitting. He gently touched their cheeks in turn, then walked away in silence. He turned around and smiled before closing the door behind him.

She had never met anyone like him before, she felt uplifted and more confident, she felt like dancing or cheering, instead she swung the baby around the floor.

As night fell Maura sneaked out of the nursery on one of her regular raids to the library. The raid itself gave her a feeling of excitement, as she crept around dark corners in constant fear of discovery. She had no time to choose the books she read, it was a matter of grabbing a couple and making a dash back along the corridor to the safety of the nursery.

She quietly turned the knob of the library door as usual, first checking the empty silent corridors before opening it. She took two books from a shelf, then replaced them with the two she had read. The sound of footsteps accompanied by the jingle of keys made her jump in fright. She slid back along the wall and behind the drapes with her heart pounding in her ears.

The door opened. From her hiding place Maura sensed her presence, then to her astonishment she heard Ethel Hanley's voice. "I should have accepted your first offer, damn you to hell Jefferson. I'll teach them a lesson yet, by God I will."

Maura listened to her angry ranting for a minute or so. 'Who is she talking to?' she mused. Plucking up courage she slid back along the wall, and peered out the side of the curtain. Ethel Hanley stood alone in front of the painting of a man. It was the same painting that Maura saw on her previous visits, when she had imagined the deep blue eyes watching her as she took the books.

'My God she is talking to a picture,' she thought in astonishment as she watched and listened from her hiding place. She continued talking to herself, shouting obscenities at times, and at others muttering inaudibly. At last she turned to go to Maura's great relief. She listened as the sound of the jingling keys faded away before emerging from her hiding place.

The nursery door burst open the following morning, just as Maura had finished bathing David. Ethel Hanley's face was black with rage.

"Just what have you been saying to Mr. Jefferson?" she screeched at Maura.

"I don't know what you are talking about," Maura said stunned by the sudden venomous outburst.

"Don't come the innocent with me. You don't mean to tell me that the contraption in the hall is not your doing," she spat.

"Oh, you must mean the baby carriage. Mr. Jefferson did say he would get it for David. I'm so glad, it's come. I will take him out for a walk as soon as I get him dressed." Maura kept her voice firm, trying not to show her fear.

"That child is not going outside this room." I am in charge here, just in case you have forgotten." She shook with rage.

Maura stared straight back at her and in as firm a voice as she could manage said.

"Miss Hanley you may be in charge of the house, but I am responsible for this child," she continued. "And I say he needs fresh air, I am taking him out in a few minutes in his new baby carriage, which his uncle kindly bought for him. Good day to you," she added as she walked past her with the baby in her arms.

Miss Hanley followed her down the front stairs. Maura tried to close her ears to her threats, but she had a hunch that she meant trouble for her.

The sound of the carriage wheels were like music to Maura's ears as she pushed the baby along the avenue. She felt as the sailors of Ulysses must have felt, when freed of Circe's spell. A motor car pulled up along side them, Andrew Jefferson jumped out of the back seat.

"Well, the top of the morning to you both," he said in a mock Irish brogue. I'm glad to see you both out in the fresh air. Is the baby carriage to your satisfaction?" he asked.

"It's grand Mr. Jefferson. We both love it, don't we," she said smiling down at the baby. "I had a bit of trouble with Miss Hanley, she tried to stop me leaving the house."

"I guessed she would give you trouble, that's why I came. I was about to rescue you, but I see you managed to

escape by yourself. Don't let her frighten you. I am glad
you stood up to her. As I said before she should have got
her marching orders long ago," he continued a note of
concern creeping into his voice. "Enough about Hanley, I
will show you where the park is."
When he had directed her to the park he got back into the
car and was gone.

Maura sat on the park bench listening to the birds sing, and
taking in deep breaths of the soft balmy, early, autumn air.

All around were people, real people, strolling, talking
and laughing. As Maura watched them her spirits soared,
she felt alive again, and a renewed stirring of the joy of
being alive came from deep within.

Ethel Hanley back in her sitting room was burning
with rage following her encounter with Maura. Her fifty-
year reign in control of the Jefferson house seemed to be
slipping away from her. 'When did It all start to go
wrong?' she asked herself. Her thoughts went back to the
time David Jefferson senior died, and her position in the
house began to die with him. Her thoughts again went
away back when she was just a young, house maid, and she
first attracted the attention of the her wealthy employer.
She had willingly shared his bed, right up until she read
about his engagement in the newspaper. After all these
years the bitterness she felt was as strong as ever.

"Marrying Miss Emily Hatton will increase his
standing in the community, why, they are one of the

wealthiest families in New York," the cook proudly told the servants in the kitchen that lunchtime, as she read the announcement from the newspaper.

She had made an excuse to leave, she felt physically sick at first, then came the anger, 'I'll show him, nobody uses me like that and gets away with it.'

She waited for him in the library the following evening, When at last he showed up she confronted him.

The encounter that followed between them was as clear in her mind as ever, almost fifty years on.

"Where the hell did you come from?" he had asked her in annoyance.

"You are to be married I hear? and you didn't think it worthwhile to tell me, you just used me," she spat. I wonder what Miss Emily Hatton would think if she knew your dirty little secret, eh?"

She watched the colour leave his face.

"What do you want, how much?"

"You can't buy me off that easy, you think your damned money buys everything, well you are wrong." Her words came out slow and menacing. "If I am to keep my mouth shut you will do what I say."

"So I am to be blackmailed, and as for the dirty little secret, as you called it, I didn't hear you objecting to it."

"Either you do what I say, or I will pay your well bred fiancée and her family a visit. Please yourself" she added.

"All right, all right, spit it out, what do you want?"

"I am staying on in this house, I'm not leaving. You will get rid of the housekeeper, and I will take over her job. At an increased salary of course" she added. Barely stopping for breath she continued. "I want no interference from you or anyone else, I will run things my way." She took pleasure at seeing the fear in his eyes as he listened to her terms. There was a long silence before he answered.

"Very well. You leave me no alternative, I will have to agree to your terms. Blackmailers usually come to a sad end," he added looking at her with contempt as he held the door open. "Go on get out of my sight" he said slamming the door after her.

Ethel watched the old housekeeper leave in tears. From that day on she ruled the house, anyone who crossed her path always regretted it. The new Mrs. Jefferson disliked Ethel from the start. Her attempts to be rid of her always ended in failure, much to her frustration.

"That woman is a menace, she seems to take pleasure in tormenting the staff. Another young maid left in tears today, you must get rid of her David," she would say.

"I can't, I promised her a home here, please don't ask me to explain, I promised that's all," he would say lamely. Emily Jefferson was a kind caring soul, who hated to see the young members of her staff made so unhappy, and being powerless to do anything about it. She had on several occasions given her notice to leave.

"Mr. Jefferson hired me so only he can fire me," she always answered.

But her best efforts to persuade her husband to get rid of her always led to an argument, and more unhappiness.

"But why, the woman is a menace to me and everyone else in the house," she had pleaded. "What hold has she got on you?"

"Please Emily, be patient, trust me, I just can't get rid of her, not yet," he would say unhappily.

Emily always had to drop the matter, she loved her husband dearly and couldn't bear to see him look so troubled, as was always the case when Hanley's name was mentioned. But Emily Jefferson was no fool, and she always had a hunch that her husband's housekeeper was blackmailing him for some reason. She was not to find the truth until much later, when she knew that he was dying.

Three days after the funeral Emily Jefferson gave Ethel her notice to leave.

"I am ordering you to leave this house, get your belongings together and go," she demanded.

"I will go if you wish, but I think you should hear what I have to say first. Now you don't want that grand appreciating notice that appeared in The New York Times ruined by scandal now do you?" she continued with a sarcastic grin on her face. "What would his two fine sons think, it would ruin them."

"I already know what you are going to tell me," Emily interrupted. "It's hardly a hanging offence. I knew all along that you were blackmailing him." He didn't tell me until he was on his death-bed, he asked me to forgive him. It was easy to forgive his one indiscretion, and I did so willingly." Her eyes narrowed to slits.

"Well it's up to you I'm sure, if you want all that scandal in the newspapers, then go ahead throw me out" she added, shrugging her shoulders.

Emily Jefferson's anger and frustration at her blackmailing tactics lasted for weeks, she wanted to be rid of her. But she feared her, knowing she was capable of destroying the family's good name. When David junior announced his engagement it gave her the excuse she needed to leave. Her grief was too raw, she just couldn't face up to the possibility of scarring the name of the man she had loved. She settled down in her new home to live out her days with Andrew, her youngest son whom she adored. But the name of Hanley was to rear its head again casting a shadow over her.

"Do you know mother, that poor grandson of yours has not been out of the nursery since he was born, until today. And the young girl that he hired to look after him, hasn't seen the light of day either. David hasn't even bothered to come to see his own son, not once in six weeks."

"Are you sure? It just doesn't sound like David. Thoughtless maybe, but not deliberately unkind." She looked troubled as Andrew went on.

"Hanley had the damned nerve to forbid the girl to take the child out. Why the hell did you or my father not get rid of that old bat long ago? She's a menace," he went on. "I have watched for years a succession of your staff leave the house. You must be renowned for the fastest turnover of servants in the entire state. And all because, of that sadist of a housekeeper. Yet, you let her stay all these years. Why, Mother, answer me that?"

He watched her stare into space. Then, slowly she turned her head to face him before, she answered.

"Son, I hoped that I wouldn't have to tell you, but I suppose I must, if only for the sake of my grandson, and the girl," she sighed.

When she had finished, there was a long silence between them.

"Now you see why I couldn't get rid of her," she said sadly.

He took her small hand in her big one, with a tremor in her voice she spoke again.

"Please don't think badly of your father, Andrew. It was just a temporary weakness, he regretted it, oh, how he regretted it. I forgave him. Can you do the same?" She looked up into her son's eyes with an expression that begged his understanding. He gently squeezed her small wrinkled hand as he spoke.

"There is nothing for me to forgive, it would take more than a careless fling to tarnish my father's name. In my memory, he will always remain an honourable, gentle giant of a man."

"Thank you son, you know it's a relief to have told

you. I should have known you above all would understand. Now you can see why Hanley will have to stay, until she dies I suppose," she said, with a tremble in her voice.

"You can't be serious? We can't let her carry on with her blackmail and torture."

"I don't see what else we can do, I tried to terminate her employment, I told you what happened," her voice trailed off into a sigh.

"We will find a way, never fear, she is not worth one of your tears. Will you promise that tomorrow you will go and see your grandson?" She nodded.

"We will go together."

Chapter 7

A Time to Forgive

No words passed between them on the journey to the graveyard, each locked in their separate thoughts.

The only sound came from the pony's steady trotting.

Sara's thoughts were still on the shadowy figure she had seen disappearing behind the pillar, she couldn't shake off the feeling of gloom. She had a premonition about it. When they reached the graveyard, Sara tied up the pony in the yard of the parochial house. An elderly priest appeared from the side door.

"Anything I can do for you?" he enquired.

"Thank you Father, but I think we can manage, we are going to the graveyard." Jean answered.

"I am just on my way over to the church, I'll walk with you. Do you know where to find the grave you are looking for?" he asked, as they walked through the church gates.

"I think I know where it is, but it has been so long, I'm not sure anymore," Jean said, her brow knitted in concentration. "Let me see, I was watching from that hill up there on the day of the funeral. I think it's over here, somewhere." She went over to the right and began searching among the headstones. The priest watched her for a minute, then followed behind her.

"If you tell me the name, I might be able to help you," he offered.

She seemed to hesitate, before answering. "Joseph Sheehey, He was drowned at sea."

The priest turned around and pointed to the left. "This way, the Sheehey's are buried over here. There is only one of that family left, she works over at Thompson's place, ... or so I've been told."

Jean nodded and followed him.

Sara watched, their bent heads, as they searched for the gravestone. Then the priest walked away, his feet crunching along the yellow gravel path. When he had gone out of sight she went over to Jean.

They stood together in silence and read the inscription on the stone.

JOSEPH SHEEHEY
DROWNED AT SEA ON THE 15th JULY, 1875
AGED 23 YEARS

Jean turned to go. Sara held her arm to steady her. The air

was still, almost as if it were holding its breath, while the two women made their way along the path. The first loud peal of the Angeles bell rang out. Sara blessed herself, her lips moving in silent prayer.

Half way up the steep hill she stopped to rest the pony, steam wafted out of his nostrils like thin smoke in the still air.

"Was Joseph Sheehey any relation of Molly's?" Sara asked, breaking the long silence.

"He was Molly's brother, I should have told you before. Now you know why, she didn't want me to come back here, the family blamed me for his death."

"Why did they blame you? Sure you didn't sink the boat," Sara asked. " And to think, that I was always trying to shield you from the sharp end of Molly's tongue. And all the time you knew rightly why she resented you."

"I'm sorry I should have been more honest about it. As to why they blamed me for the tragedy; he was trying to earn the money for our passage to Canada. His family believed that he wouldn't have taken the risk, of going out to fish on that blustery day, if it hadn't been for me."

"How did they find out about it? Your romance I mean."

"My interfering Sister-in-law. She saw us walking hand in hand on the beach, she created merry hell for us, in both camps. And you know the rest," she concluded.

When they reached the driveway the sun had disappeared behind Slieve Snaght, leaving scarlet in its wake, colouring the evening sky with a warm red glow.

Sara closed the stable door, and went around to the kitchen. Molly was seated in her chair by the range as usual. But she seemed anxious and flustered.

"Is everything all right?" Sara asked, taking off her coat.

"Aye, but you have a visitor," she pointed to the other side of the kitchen.

In the dim light Sara stared at the figure without recognition.

"Hello Sara," he said hoarsely.

She gasped out loud at the sound of his voice, then grabbed the back of a chair to support her shaking legs. Mary Kate ran over to her holding out her arms, bending down she picked her up, and flopped down on the chair.

"What do you want?" Her own voice sounded distant in her ears. As her eyes became adjusted to the gloom, she noticed how thin and gaunt he looked, he was just a shadow of the man she had last seen, scarcely two years ago.

"Like I said to Molly here, I just need to talk to you. A lot has happened, I mean you no ..." His words were cut short by a fit of coughing.

"He's a sick man Sara. I wasn't going to let him past the door, then when I saw the appearance of him...." she broke off nodding at the slumped choking figure.

Molly poured two cups of tea, and added two heaped

spoon-fulls of sugar. "Give him this. You could do with a cup yourself by the look of you."

Sara gave him the tea, then sat down to drink her own in silence. She was shocked by his frail appearance, yet she was still afraid of him.

'Why the hell did you come here?" she wanted to scream, but then a small voice from within, tugged at her conscience, and reminded her of her duty.

"Sara, I need to talk to you, on your own, then I'll be on my way." The cough had stopped and his voice was steady.

She got up from the chair still holding Mary Kate in her arms.

"We can talk up in the nursery, if It's that private. But I have no secrets from Molly." she added.

"I know. But what I have to say is only for your ears."

She lit the nursery fire with a match, before sitting down opposite him. Watching his grey pallor, as he gasped for breath after climbing the stairs, made her realise just how sick he really was. At last he began to talk.

"I want you to listen to what I have to say, then I will go and leave you in peace."

"Say what you have to then, I'm listening," she said, impatiently.

Between bouts of coughing and breathless spasms, he told her of the harrowing events of the past eighteen months. When he had finished, she said.

"I'm glad you had no cartridges, he isn't worth hanging for. I always knew Seamus was evil, even before poor Maura became his victim," she continued. "I'm just sorry that he had you fooled." She rested her face on Mary Kate's head, her tears mingling with her downy hair.

He reached over and handed her a letter.

"Post this to Maura for me. I doubt if she will forgive me, but I must try." He got up to his feet unsteadily. "I'll be on my way back to the station."

"No wait, the trains have all gone. And anyway, It's nearly dark. You can stay here tonight, I'll make a bed up for you in the wee room adjoining here," she added.
He hesitated for a moment then sat down again.

"All right, I'm in no fit state to argue. But just for tonight. I'll get the train home tomorrow."
Mary Kate had fallen asleep on her lap. He watched as Sara got her ready for bed. As she laid her gently in the cot he spoke again.

"You did right to take her, and rear her yourself. She's so like Maura at that age," he added.

"Aye she is. You know I did it all for Maura and her. I didn't want to leave, but you left me no choice."

"I know that, I know that," he repeated. Then raising his eyes dully to Sara's he said, "what a bitter lesson I have learned Sara."

That night sleep wouldn't come. She lay rigid listening to him coughing and gasping, while she turned everything he had told her over, and over in her mind. She had expected the old John Quinn to emerge from within. The memory of the day she left him was still etched on her mind. The humble apologetic man, who asked her forgiveness, bore no resemblance to the aggressive, uncompromising man who showed no mercy to his wife and only child. 'But. It wasn't all- bad, away back in the early days,' she reminded herself. 'He doted on Maura when she was a wee waine. Where did it all go wrong? And where do I go from here?' she asked herself. The haunted look in his eyes loomed up before her, as she lay staring into the blackness. 'Was I wrong to walk out on him?' she asked herself. The sound of another spasm of coughing, brought her back to the immediate problem; the state of his health. 'What if he has consumption?' She shivered at the thought of putting them all in danger of the most, dreaded of diseases. 'Dear God what am I to do?' she whispered in the darkness.

Getting up, she left the nursery and went to Jean's room. She went over to the bed and shook her awake gently.

"Whist! It's only me. I need your advice badly." The old woman sat up rubbing her eyes.

"What's the matter. Is it you Sara? It must be serious to wake me at this ungodly hour." She lit the candle by her bed, and gestured for Sara to sit down on the bed beside her.

"Put my shawl around you, you'll catch your death." Barely stopping for breath, Sara told her about John in tones of anguish. "What will I do? I can't turn him out in that condition. I can't get over the change in him, not just the sickness, he begged me to forgive him. All I can say is, he's not the man that I thought I knew," she continued. "I wouldn't feel so guilty if he was." Jean patted her arm reassuringly.

"Nobody's all good or bad; they're both, like me. You know Sara, it's hard to find out what a cruel fool you have been, in the way he did. But he has learned from it, and the truth has set him free," Jean concluded.

"Maybe I should go home and look after him, after all it is my duty. I married him, for better or for worse," she said getting up.

"Sara, you have done your duty, more than your duty."

"Thank you Jean for listening, and for your wisdom."

"Sara, if you want to look after him here, I will help you. I'm not that decrepit. I'll be of some use. I just can't imagine what life would be like here if you went. That's selfish, I know and I'm sorry, but it's true."

"I'll just go and see how he is, then I'll decide what to do," Sara said leaving the room.

The dawn was just breaking when she got back to the nursery. No sound came from the adjoining room, she listened carefully, her ear to the door. Then she turned the door handle and went in.

He was lying on his back with his eyes closed, for a few frightening seconds she thought he was dead. When she saw he was breathing, she shook him gently by the shoulder.

"John, are you all right? It's me Sara."

He opened his eyes; they had a glazed look. He stared at her blankly at first, then slowly into his eyes, came the light of recognition.

"Sara, it's you. Where did you come from?"

"You stayed here last night, it was too late to go home," she reminded him.

"Aye, it's coming back to me now, I forgot for a minute."

"There's not much time left, I better get home while I'm able," he said. He struggled to get out of the bed, before collapsing back on the pillow gasping for breath. When he recovered a little she asked.

"Have you seen a doctor?"

"Aye, he told me I don't have much time. Cancer of the lungs he says. Don't pity me Sara, I have been spared long enough to do what I had to, and now I'm ready to go."

Sara looked down at the tragic figure lying on the bed with sadness. 'It could all have been so different. If only you had listened to us. Oh, Maura, I miss you so much right now'. Looking back at him again she said.

"John you are not well enough to go home. Will you let me look after you here?"

He shook his head, "no, I must go home, I want to be laid to rest in Clougher, with my parents."

"I will see to that, trust me," she said reassuringly.

"My mother seems close to me these days, I can see her clearly at times. Do you believe me?" he asked.

"Aye, I do. Mothers are always close when you need them." She sat by his bed and held his hand, while he fell into a peaceful doze.

She heard a knock at the door, then Jean poked her head in.

"How is he?" she whispered. Sara shook her head.

"Not good," she whispered back.

They went quietly from the room on tiptoe.

"He wanted to go home, to be buried beside his mother and father. But he's too far through; he wouldn't make it."

Sara and Jean kept a vigil by his bedside for two days and nights. He slept fitfully, and at times seemed not to be conscious. Then suddenly he opened his eyes, a weak smile crossed his face. And in a voice that was barely a whisper, he said.

"Sara, I didn't deserve you, I didn't think for a minute that you would forgive. I've left the place to you. The money is all gone, just enough left to bury me."

"There is nothing to forgive, you have suffered enough. Just rest now, I won't leave you," she said, her voice choking with emotion.

She was still holding his hand in the wee hours, when he stopped breathing. She sat beside the still form in silence. Then looked down at the work worn hand, that was still entwined in her's.

'You were always so sure about everything John Quinn. Always in control; master of your own destiny. I never thought I would live to see you so humbled.'

Her tears fell silently down her face and onto the sheet that covered his motionless chest.

Jean put her hand on her shoulder. "It's over Sara. He has found his way into the comfort of God's presence. And he was fortunate enough, and wise enough to have learned from his mistakes." She gently prised Sara's hand from his.

"Come Sara, you can do no more, you need to sleep."

His remains were taken, to Clougher by train, where the hearse was waiting to take him the last mile. Jean and James Thompson came with her. Together with his neighbours and friends, they walked the last mile, to his resting- place.

Chapter 8

A New Understanding

The wind beat around Sara's bent body as she struggled breathlessly up the lane towards the thatched farmhouse. As the house drew near she stopped to rest, then apprehensively walked the last few yards. The walls, that she had once white washed with pride, were now a mix of the brown and green mildew of neglect. The place had a sad lonely air, from which she wanted to escape. The key was under the bucket where it was always hidden; she half hoped it wouldn't be there. 'I will have to go in, after coming all this way it would be stupid and cowardly not to,' she reasoned with herself. The door opened with a reluctant creek. The damp cold odour of rot, and dirt made her shudder. It was hard to imagine the cosy clean haven that had once been her domain, and her pride. Here she had cooked and cleaned and entertained her neighbours.

A mouse scurried across the floor, as if to mock her presence. On the mantle-shelf she spied John's pipe. Then her eyes were drawn to his gun leaning against the brace, where he had left it. Shivers ran up and down her spine, she tore her eyes away from it. 'I can't bear to think of him sitting waiting for Seamus, with murder in his heart,' she whispered to the emptiness. The lower room brought her even less comfort than the kitchen, the same damp rotting odour entered her nostrils. Then her eyes were drawn to a familiar looking object lying under the sideboard. She bent down and picked it up; the button eyes of Maura's old, and once much loved, ragdoll stared back at her. Sitting down on the damp arm -chair, she let the pent up tears slide down her face. 'You are a fool, a crazy fool, this place can never be home again.'

A knock at the door made her jump in alarm, she reluctantly went to the kitchen door, and breathed a sigh of relief when she saw Grace Murphy standing there.

"I didn't mean to frighten you, I saw you from the window,"

"Come in, it's cold and damp in here, mind you at least it gets you out of the rain."

"Come down to our place and get warm, I'll make you a cup of tea. I didn't get a chance to say much to you at the funeral. I have the place to myself for a change."

"Thanks Grace. I have stayed here long enough anyway." She locked the door with relief, grateful that Grace had given her the excuse she needed to get away. The warm kitchen and hot tea helped to restore her a little.

"Did John tell you what went on... about him? Seamus I mean. She fiddled nervously with her wedding ring as she spoke.

"Aye, he told me everything and I'm sorry, poor wee Ellen. I feel guilty, I could have warned you."

"You know I used to lie awake at nights wondering how I could get revenge. God forgive me, I wanted to kill the evil bastard with my bare hands."

"I know, I wanted to do the same, but then it would have been talked about through the nine glens, and Ellen would have been in a worse fix. The whole thing has to be kept a secret, even her father mustn't find out," she spoke in a hushed tone, bending her head close to Sara with fear in her eyes.

"Don't worry Grace, that secret will go to the grave with me."

"What is it, that it says in the bible... *revenge is mine, I will repay.* We will have to leave it in God's hands."

"Aye, you're right Sara. But we would need to pray to God that wherever he is....the Almighty will protect any wee girls, that crosses his path."

"Isn't life a strange puzzle, I lay awake many a night listening to Maura cry, and like I said I wanted to kill him. But out of all that came Mary Kate and she is everything in the world to me now. Do you know Grace, the two old women back at the rectory fuss over her like mother hens. They even fight about who is going to do what for her."

"I can well believe it" Grace said with a grin.

"Let me pour you another cup. I don't remember when I enjoyed a gossip as much. It has helped me to talk about that awful business. It's hard keep a secret like that." Sara gave her a look of understanding.

"I came here today because, I thought that I could turn it into a home again for us. I even wrote to Maura, asking her to come home. But too much has happened, it just wouldn't work."

"Give it time, things might seem different in a month or two," Grace said.

"Maybe you're right, time might heal. Do you know the thing that bothers me most? What will I tell Mary Kate about her father? She's bound to ask one day. She looked at Grace with sorrowful eyes that begged an answer."

"If it were me, I would see no sin in telling a white lie. No, no sin at all," she answered with a sympathetic smile.

Later when they said their goodbyes on the doorstep, Grace kissed Sara on the cheek, they were united by a bond of shared grief that needed no words.

The rain was coming down in sheets when she stepped onto the station platform. Then she saw him, standing in the doorway of the waiting room, the collar of his grey overcoat turned up around his ears. His greying hair bunched out above the collar of his coat. He smiled as she walked towards him, his blue-grey eyes looked kinder than she had ever seen them.

"The train is late as usual," he greeted her. "It's an awful evening to trudge up that hill with the wind in your face."

"It's very good of you to come to meet me Mr. Thompson. I could have walked it, I feel bad about taking you out on a night like this."

"Think nothing of it. Anyway, Aunt Jean was worried about you." He handed her a rug when they got into the trap. "This might keep some of the rain off you."

"Thanks," she said.

They remained silent until he stopped to rest the pony, half way up the steep hill.

"How were things at Clougher?" he asked.

"Lonely. Lonely, and cold. The house was as cold as the grave, it all looked so neglected."

"Aunt Jean told me he left the place to you."

"Aye he did. But I'm not sure what to do with it. I thought I did until today, it just didn't feel like home anymore."

"Houses in this God-awful damp climate go to rack and ruin very quick, as you found out at the rectory."

"It's not just the damp, I could soon put that to rights. Like I said it just wasn't home anymore."

"Well, I'm glad. That sounds selfish, but we need you."

"Get on up, there Prince." The pony moved on up the hill and turned into the drive.

When Sara saw the house appear dark and sombre against the dark and rainy sky, she felt at ease.

'I'm home,' she whispered to herself. When she opened

the kitchen door she was surprised to find it empty. She took off her wet coat and hung it on a hook in the front hall. Then she heard Molly's voice coming from the direction of the drawing room. She looked baffled. 'What is she doing in there? We haven't sat in there since the time Mr. Thompson disappeared, and we thought he was gone for good.' Going over to the door she opened it, and peered inside. To her amazement Molly and Jean sat at either side of a blazing fire, each deep in conversation. When she left that morning they seemed as hostile to one another as ever. 'I wonder what brought this on?' she thought. She cleared her throat loudly, making them aware of her presence.

"Sara dear you're back, I'm so glad," Jean said getting up from her chair. Mary Kate ran to greet her, her chubby arms above her head. "Nana, Nana," she shouted excitedly.

"You must be wet through, come and sit here. I'll go and get you some hot tea," Jean said scurrying from the room.

"Well Molly, out with it. What's all this about?"

"Me sitting in here with the enemy you mean. Well, when you left this morning, we were both worried that you might go back to Clougher, for good." She looked away sheepishly before going on, "so we decided to bury the hatchet. If we had any hope of you staying at all, we would have to stop bickering."

"I'm glad to hear it. I'm very fond of you both."

"She decided that it was stupid for her to sit in here on her own, so we will have a bit of comfort from now on. So now you have it," she concluded taking a deep breath. Just then Jean came in with a tray for Sara.

"I could get used to this kind of pampering, thank you both for everything," she said softly.

A loud noise woke Sara from a heavy doze. She scrambled out of bed still half- asleep. Throwing a shawl over her shoulders she went out to the corridor to investigate. The smell of burning set alarm bells ringing in her head. Then she saw a light coming from under the door of the locked room. She ran across the corridor and turned the handle, to her great relief it opened. The floor carpet was alight and from the light the fire was creating she could see an oil lamp lying broken on the floor with flames leaping all around it. Then to her horror she saw him lying on the floor a few inches from the flames. In a flash she was across the room. She pulled him across the floor and out the door. With her shawl she beat at the flames frantically, then grabbing the bedspread she threw it on top of the burning carpet choking it, and leaving her in complete darkness.

She lit the nursery lamp, and went back to where he was lying. "Mr. Thompson, Mr. Thompson," she shouted shaking him by the shoulders. "Are you all right, for God's sake answer me?" She put her ear to his chest. He was still breathing, much to her relief. Then he began to moan. 'At least you're alive,' she said out loud.

"What happened, what's wrong?" Jean's voice came from behind her.

"A fire. He's still alive. He might be more, drunk, than burned. Will you stay with him while I go and make sure the fire is out?" With the lamp in her hand, she went back into the room.

It still smelled of smoke but the flames had gone out. Raising the lamp up high she looked around the room. To her surprise it looked like a room where the occupant had just left. Everything from the hairbrush on the dressing table to the painting of a beautiful woman above the fireplace, gave her the feeling that she was about to return at any moment. Shivers ran down her spine, 'I feel like someone has just walked over my grave,' she whispered as she walked out and shut the door behind her.

"How is he?" she asked Jean. I'm not sure, but I think he is just drunk." Sara shook him again.

"Mr. Thompson, are you all right?"

"Leave me alone," he muttered.
Sara helped him to his feet, and steadied him along the corridor, and back to his room. Jean helped her to get him into bed. They could see no sign of burns on his body, so they left him to sleep while they went down to the kitchen.

It was much later before Sara realised that her hands were burned. As the shock of the fire wore off, she was seized by pain. Jean looked horrified when she saw her red and blistered skin.

"We will have to get a doctor, I will go myself as soon as it's light."

"No, don't make a fuss they will be all right," Sara protested.

"What was he thinking about anyway? We could all have been burned alive. Sara once again we are in your debt."

"I'm glad I got it out in time, that's all," she replied through gritted teeth.

"I'm going to get medical help for you it's obvious you're in agony."

"No, I'll be all right. The pain will soon go."
But she had gone out the door, before Sara could stop her. Just half an hour later she was back in the yard with the doctor.

"You will have to rest these hands for a week or more, they are badly burned," the doctor warned her, as he finished putting on the bandages.

"I suppose I'll have no option if I must wear these bandages," she said with a sigh. For the first time since she could remember her hands were idle. Each time she offered her help in the kitchen she was ordered to sit and rest.

"Everything is under control, we are managing fine," Jean said.

"Aye, we are doing all right," Molly chipped in.

"I'm not an invalid, I could help you with something surely," Sara protested.

"Will you hold your whist, and take the waine out for a walk when you have the chance."

The two old women in an agreeable mood took a bit of getting used to for Sara. Mr. Thompson had not appeared since the fire. But Jean assured her he was all right. "He is making himself scarce. He feels very bad about what happened," Jean informed her. "I tried to tell him about the drink. It will be the death of him yet. But it went in one ear and out the other," she said, with a shake of her head.

Sara helped Mary Kate into her new coat; an early Christmas present from Maura. She walked up and down the floor like a miniature model. "Nice Nana," she said rubbing the new coat with her tiny hands. Sara smiled with pleasure as she put on the woollen hat that she had knitted for her. "I love you Mary Kate," she whispered kissing the top of her head.

Outside the sun shone brightly, making the biting cold east wind come as a shock to the senses. They walked along the cliff path and down towards the shore. Sara found a sheltered spot under a hill, and sat down. Below on the beach, the wind blew the waves into a frenzy. She watched as they crashed and foamed against the rocks in a wild fury. 'I have never before had time just to stop and stare,' she thought to herself. The wild beauty of the day made her feel exhilarated. Then she saw him climbing the path below her, he struggled, head bent against the wind.

Mary Kate ran to greet him, before she had time to stop her. "Hello there wee lady," he said lifting her up. He stopped in front of Sara, holding the child in his arms.

"Good morning. How are the hands?"

"Healing well, and the pain has gone out of them."

"Good, good," he repeated clearing his throat self-consciously. "You have probably guessed that I have been avoiding you. I'm ashamed of myself. I don't remember much about it to be honest. The whiskey, or as Molly would say the Devil's buttermilk." He sat down beside her, with Mary Kate on his knee. They sat in silence for a few minutes. His eyes stared vacantly ahead, his face a reddish-purple colour from the cold wind.

"I know you are wondering what the Hell I was doing, ... in that room drunk in the middle of the night."

"It's your business Mr. Thompson. You don't have to explain anything to me."

"For God's sake woman, I nearly burned you all in your beds. And you say it's not your business. I bet this child would have greeted me with a kick, if she were old enough to know that I could have killed her. It's strange how a man will grab for reasons to excuse the bad things he does."

"I only know one thing," Sara said. "It wasn't intended as a bad deed. You are not a bad man, that's all," she added.

"Maybe not, but I'm a danger to others. And, as for me. I am of no use, to myself or anyone else. I would be no loss," he added with a shrug of his shoulders.

"Why do you have so little faith in yourself, you are always doing yourself down?"

"What is there to have faith in? I simply wasn't worth risking your life to save. The night my wife died in childbirth, I went to Ballyneely for a Doctor. I had to wake him up out of a drunken stuper, and half carry him to the trap. Is it any wonder she died? And do you wonder why I blame myself?"

"It wasn't your fault that the doctor was drunk. And even if he had been sober, it might have made no difference. Can you not accept it as God's will?"

"I stopped believing in God long ago." He gave her a look of pained despair.

"But he hasn't stopped believing in you," she said quietly, her eyes soft and pleading.

"I have no answer to that, except to say that if God does exist, and believes in the likes of me, he must have patience to burn. There are only two things, no..., three things, that might make me believe in a higher power. Do you want to know what they are?" She nodded. "Kindly forgiving people like you, the trusting innocence of this lovely little being and all the beauty of nature." He looked away from the child, and gazed out at the billowing sea as he spoke. "I must get back to the house," he said getting to his feet. "I have to get the fuel in for the fires, and milk the cow. Aunt Jean put me in charge of a few of your chores. And if you ask me I got off lightly," he said with a sheepish grin.

"I'll soon be back in harness. The days are so long with nothing to do."

"Don't. You need a rest, as do those burned hands of yours. And, anyway it's doing me good to be useful for a change. Thanks for the chat. You have given me a lot to think about." He rubbed Mary Kate's curls, before walking off towards the house.

Back in the nursery, Sara began to read Maura's old letters. As she read, she couldn't help noticing how much more cheerful her recent letters had become, compared with the earlier ones. She decided to tear up the letter she had ready for posting, in which she had begged her to come home. It was too emotional, too raw. 'I should have waited until time helped me to see things in a better light. It was unfair to burden Maura with all her earlier feeling of guilt.' In this new frame of mind she began a new letter.

'I will tell her the farm is hers if she wants it,' she told herself before she began writing.

In the cot Mary Kate was still fast asleep, her thumb in her mouth. Impulsively, Sara snipped off one of her downy curls and put it in the envelope, then adding John's letter she sealed it.

From the window she watched James Thompson walking across the yard with a bucket in his hand, and then disappeared into the byre to milk the cow.

'I wonder if he locked the room again?' she suddenly

thought. She had a compelling desire to find out. She turned the handle, and it opened with a creak. The interior amazed her once more. It showed no signs of neglect in the way the rest of the house had. No cobwebs mildew or dust in sight. The carpet and bedspread had burn-holes. But instead of a lingering smell of the fire, there was a scent of lavender. She stood before the portrait, and gazed admiringly at the loveliness of the young woman, as she smiled down at her from the wall. She looked around the room once more. No, she had not imagined the room looking as though its occupant had just popped out for a minute, it was all too disturbingly real. There was a large wardrobe running the full length of one wall, gingerly she opened it. There were rows of women's clothing hanging neatly in line, closing the wardrobe door she walked over to the dressing table. A mother of pearl brush and comb lay on top. She opened the jewel case and looked inside. Then taking out a beautiful gold locket, she turned it over, and read the inscription;

ALL MY LOVE. JAMES. DECEMBER 8th, 1915.

A writing desk stood at the window, on the top there was a fountain pen and note paper as if waiting to be used by its owner. She sat down at the desk and looked out at the stormy ocean, and beyond to the purple-brown hills.

'She had everything to live for, had Mrs. James Thompson. A husband who loved her, a child who would have been adored, and all the beauty of nature at her best,' she whispered. She got up from the chair and quietly left the room to its sad ghosts.

Chapter 9

Christmas 1927

The dark winter days passed slowly. Sara spent most of the short afternoons carrying in fuel for the fires. She had just lit the study fire when James Thompson walked in. One glance at him told her that he had been drinking heavily again. The all too familiar bleary eyes, and unshaven face spoke for itself.

"Good morning," she ventured.

"What's good about it?" he muttered reaching for the whiskey bottle.

She watched as he gulped down the whiskey, holding the glass with shaking hands.

"Aunt Jean wants me to take her down to the village. But I'm not up to it, as you can see," he said. Sara was silent.

"Well...?"

"Oh, all right, I'll go. But, on one condition."

"Making conditions now are we?" he asked sarcastically.

"Yes I am," she answered, her voice raised in annoyance.

"If I am to go to Ballyneely, then you will have to fill the turf baskets, and do the milking."

"Go to Hell. Who do you think you are, giving me orders?"

"I'm not giving you orders Mr. Thompson. But I can't do everything." He stared at her with an angry gaze, which made her feel uncomfortable.

Suddenly, the anger left him. He lowered his head into his shaking hands in silence. Sara's anger turned to pity as she watched him in helpless silence.

"I'm not in good shape today, as I'm sure you have guessed," he said with a short laugh.

"So I see," she said lamely. "Don't bother about the turf, I'll do it myself in the evening."

"No you won't. It will do me good to do something." He poured out more of the whiskey into the glass, while Sara watched in dismay. "Golden liquid, it works like magic. See... I have stopped shaking," he held out his steady hand as proof of his statement.

"The stuff is only killing you. Like Molly says, it's the Devil's buttermilk. Now you are going to tell me it's none of my damned business."

"It's none of your damned business," he repeated.

"I'll go and get the pony yoked. I can see I am wasting my breath," she said getting up to go.

"Wait. I'm sorry. I have tried to keep away from

this bloody stuff. But I don't seem to be able to do without it. It creates in me, a state of amnesia....a temporary way to escape the black mist that constantly surrounds me. Do you know what I'm talking about?" he asked, with a sense of urgency in his tone.

"Aye I think maybe I do, and I'm sorry for you. But you must know that it's hard for them that care about you, to watch you destroying yourself. But like you said, it's none of my business." She gave him a look of pity before leaving the room.

The Ballyneely shops were all aglow displaying their wares, and decorations for Christmas. Jean stopped at Murphy's window to admire the coats on display.

"I like the grey one, what about you?" she asked Sara.

"The blue one with the fur trimming I think," Sara said.

An hour later Jean was ready to go, much to Sara's relief. She enjoyed getting away from the house for a while. But she was worried about leaving Mary Kate with Molly. The old woman was becoming less, and less mobile with each day that passed. She was pleased when Jean eventually appeared out of Murphys ready to go home. She was carrying just one small parcel. 'It took you long enough to buy one item,' Sara said to herself as she anxiously waited to get on her way.

They turned into the drive just before four o'clock. Darkness was already closing in as they reached the house. Molly sat in her usual corner by the range.

"Everything all right?" she enquired.

"I'm that glad your back, it's the waine, she's not well. She woke up crying, and when I felt her she was burning up."

Sara's heart pounded in her throat, as fear seized her. She lifted her from Molly's lap, and almost froze. She felt limp and her tiny face looked pasty-white, and yet her skin felt hot and feverish.

"What can be wrong with her. Oh, God please don't let anything happen to her?" she said in a shaky voice filled with anguish.

"The doctor will be here soon," James said from the doorway. "He's out on a call at the Malloney's, the housekeeper told me. I went there, and told him."

"Thank you," she said in a trembling voice, not taking her eyes from the small pale face.

"I'll get Aunt Jean" he said leaving the kitchen.

In the nursery Dr. Mallin examined her in silence, while Sara looked on anxiously.

"She is very sick and has a high fever. But to be frank, I'm not sure what caused it. It's a virus of some kind. Just try and get as much fluid into her as possible..... and pray," he added before leaving.

As the night wore on, and she showed no sign of improvement, Sara became frantic with worry.

"I think it's, measles," Jean said. "I only experienced it once, when James was an infant. Are you willing to try whiskey?" she asked Sara.

"All right, I suppose it's worth trying," she replied hesitantly.

"This is one occasion when James's whiskey might come in useful," Jean said as she measured out a small quantity, and made punch. She tried in vain to persuade the child to drink it voluntarily.

"I don't like doing this pet. But I'll have to be cruel to be kind." She held her nose and put the cup to her lips, thus forcing her to swallow the liquid.

"Good girl, it's gone down," she said while Mary Kate cried and spluttered in protest. Sara must have dozed off momentarily.

"There are spots behind her ears. Look!" Jean Thompson's excited voice made her jump out of her stuper in alarm.

"What is it, what's wrong," she stammered.

"The spots have started to come out," she repeated. Lifting her out of the cot, Sara looked behind her ears. Sure enough, bright red spots were beginning to appear.

"Thank God," she said with relief.

"And thank James' whiskey, I knew it would come in useful one day," Sara looked at her with a broad smile.

"Aye," she said. "I don't think I can call it the Devil's buttermilk anymore."

In the kitchen Sara found Molly slumped in her chair, with her head bent forward.

"Molly, wake up. Why aren't you in bed?"

"Oh, it's you," she said. Then suddenly memory seemed to return.

"The waine, how is she?" There was anxiety in her tone. "She is a wee bit better. It's the measles. You should be in your bed," she added.

"I couldn't sleep anyway. I was that worried," tears filled her eyes as she spoke. As she helped her to bed, Sara felt a warm sense of caring love for the inhabitants of Redland's Rectory. When she thought about the reason for her being here, it was all the more amazing. She had been ruled by an instinctive desire to keep a promise, hastily made to her daughter and with an overwhelming need to protect Mary Kate from the harsh life of an orphanage, had driven her blindly to seek refuge in the old house. Now she was amazed at the protective affection, and caring shown to them both by Molly, Jean, and even more surprisingly, James Thompson.

Mary Kate recovered rapidly during the following days which was in the run up to Christmas.

The kitchen became the centre of the preparations for the festive season. Molly baked cakes and puddings, leaving a delicious aroma, which penetrated every corner of the house. Mary Kate delighted in watching Molly as she worked at the big table, and occasionally sampling the cake mixtures when she got Molly's back turned.

James appeared to be sober during the day at least. Sara watched him going in and out of the workshop at the back of the house with curiosity.

Jean was also acting mysteriously, spending hours alone in her room. One morning she came into the kitchen and announced that, the drawing room was out of bounds until Christmas.

"Sara do you know where I could get holly with berries on?" she enquired.

"Aye, there's plenty down in Mona glen. I noticed it last winter when I was hunting for firewood. I'll go down and get some in the afternoon, if you like," she offered.

"What is the old tarter up to I wonder" Molly commented as soon as she went.

"Things couldn't be as bad as they were last winter, no matter what. It was a miracle that we didn't die of hunger," Sara reminded her.

In the late afternoon Sara made her way down to the glen. She broke off the branches of prickly holly, with its blood red berries, and put it in the sack.

When she climbed to the top of the hill she stopped, and looked back down towards the valley with its whitewashed farm cottages tucked neatly under the low hills. Turf smoke wafted out of the chimneys, and scented the crisp winter air. In three days time, on the eve of Christmas, a lighted candle would shine from each window to welcome the birth of Christ. A feeling of joy and hope sent her spirits soaring, as she experienced a new understanding of the meaning of Christmas.

When Sunday Mass ended on Christmas Eve, Sara was leaving the church, when she heard Father Mc Laughlin calling her name.

"Did you want me for something Father?" she asked.

"Yes, I want a few words with you. I had hoped to see you on Friday, when I was at the rectory with Molly. Will you come up to the house?"

She nodded and followed him into the parochial house. He pointed to a chair by the fire. They sat facing each other in silence for a few seconds, his bushy eyebrows knitted together, as he stared at her. She felt uncomfortable under his stern gaze. He cleared his throat nervously and began.

"This is a rather delicate matter, brought to my notice by one of my parishioners. And, as your Parish Priest I am obliged to discuss it with you. It is a matter of your moral welfare," he went on.

Sara became even more puzzled as she listened. 'What in the devil is he getting at?' she wondered.

"I have been told that you left your husband, and went to live at the rectory with Mr. Thompson. Is this true?" he asked searching her face with a fixed gaze.

"I did leave my husband, and I went to work for Mr. Thompson. My granddaughter and myself have lived there ever since. But what this has to do with my moral welfare, has me baffled."

He cleared his throat again before answering. "Mrs. Quinn, you must surely be aware, of how people talk about such matters in a small community like this one."

She got up from her chair, her whole being seized by anger.

"I thought that you were above listening to idle gossip and lies. What others might think, drove me from my home in the first place. And do you know Father, I couldn't care less about what others might think." She sat down in the chair again and gave him a long angry stare. "I have every reason to be grateful to Mr. Thompson and his Aunt. They gave me a home when I needed it. I have done nothing wrong, nothing to be ashamed of."

"No need to raise your voice." His face reddened with annoyance, his bushy eyebrows, moving up and down as he spoke.

"If you have done nothing to feel ashamed of, then so be it..."

He raised his hands, palms up in Sara's direction, to silence her before going on.

"I'm sorry if I have upset you, but it was my duty to tell you about what is being said," he said, in a softer tone. "Put the matter out of your head. It's all part of the price we have to pay, for living in a small community," he said getting up and opening the door for her.

"Good day to you Father," she said dryly, as she shot a look of indignation in his direction.

On the road home she was still consumed with a roaring rage that would not be still. In this frame of mind she met a sober James Thompson on the driveway. He was bent under the weight of a large pine tree, as he half carried, half pulled it along.

"Want a hand?" she offered.

"I'll manage. The bloody thing would tear the hands off you. Damned needles," he said rubbing his hands against his trousers. "Don't tell Jean you have seen the confounded thing. It's supposed to be a surprise." He sat down on the ditch and began plucking pine needles out of his hands.

"What's up with you. You look very glum for someone just coming from worship," he said, peering up at her.

"Oh, it's nothing," she said, looking away from his gaze.

"Something's bothering you. Come on out with it."

She sat down on the ditch beside him and told him about her encounter with the Priest.

"I'm that mad. I'm sorry I shouldn't have told you. You are the last person I should have told."

He gave a short dry laugh before he spoke again.

"Sara…..wise, caring, unselfish Sara." He gave her a long hard stare.

"Do you really care about a few stupid gossips, who have nothing better to do? Well do you?" he demanded.

"Put that way, no, I don't. But that doesn't mean I'm

not mad." When she looked at him again he had a broad grin on his face. Before she could stop herself, she burst out laughing.

"Do you know, that is the first time I have ever heard you laugh," he said. "Now we better get this damned monster up to the house. You can carry the trunk end of it," he said. "You see it for the first time on Christmas morning," he reminded her as they set off.

On Christmas morning Sara dressed Mary Kate, before going down to the kitchen. Molly was already up, and had the range alight.

"Happy Christmas, Sara, and Happy Christmas to you Mary Kate." Look pet, Santa Claus has been," she pointed to the red stocking hanging from the mantle shelf. "Nana, Nana, Santa bring me presents," she cried excitedly, as she pulled a doll out of the stocking. They both watched her happy excited wee face, with smiles of pleasure.

"Happy Christmas to you all," Jean greeted them, poking her head into the kitchen.

"The goose smells appetising," she said, sniffing the air. Mary Kate ran to show her what Santa Claus brought her. She kissed her affectionately, then clearing her throat she began.

"I want you all in the drawing room, in about half an hour. I'll call when I'm ready. Oh, and by the way, we are all eating in the dining room today! And one more thing.

When lunch is over, I will take over the kitchen work for the rest of the day."

"Well that's a turn up for the books," Molly commented when she went out.

"Miss Thompson requests the pleasure of your company, right away." James announced. When the door was opened, the tree stood in all it's glory, lighted by dozens of tiny candles.

"Merry Christmas to one and all," James greeted them. Mary Kate made a dash for the tree, and gazed at it with wonder in her eyes.

"It's lovely. Thank you, from all of us." Sara said turning to Jean.

"James deserves some credit as well. He brought the tree home."

"It's a good tree, isn't it?" James said, winking at Sara.

"Aye, it's a grand tree. Thanks to both of you," Jean smiled with pleasure.

"Now, she said. Sit down, and I will distribute the presents." She nodded in James's direction as she spoke.

"Your present comes first Molly. It wouldn't fit under the tree." James wheeled in a chair, and positioned it in front of Molly. "This should give you some mobility." He sat down in it, and manoeuvred it around in circles with his hands, to demonstrate. Mary Kate ran over to him.

"Me, me ride," she cried with her arms in the air.

"Where to Madam?" he asked, lifting her onto his knee. He went to the door and back. Then he stopped in front of Molly.

"Your turn Molly." She grabbed his hand and kissed it.

"Oh thank you, thank you," she said with tearful emotion. "I couldn't have wished for anything better. God bless you both." Sara helped her into the chair, and with steady hands she began to manoeuvre herself around the room. "It's grand, I will be able to get outside again in the spring, that's if God spares me." Her old face was aglow with pleasure as she anticipated the new freedom that lay before her.

The gifts from under the tree were distributed to each of them. When Sara opened her large parcel, she found the grey coat with the fur trimming, that she had admired in Murphy's window.

"I don't know what to say, I'm speechless. It's lovely, thank you."

James Thompson stayed sober for most of Christmas day, much to everyone's delight. In the late afternoon he came into the drawing room.

"Santa Claus left this on the doorstep for you," he said to Mary Kate. Taking her by the hand, he led her into the hallway. Everyone followed to see what it was, when they heard the child's squeals of delight. The most beautiful and exquisitely made dolls- house sat in the hall. Each room was furnished with miniature furniture.

"He made it for her himself," Jean whispered.

Sara felt her eyes fill with tears. 'So this is what he was doing in the shed.' Molly's words on the day of her arrival in the house now resounded in her ears. 'His bark is worse than his bite' she had said. When Mary Kate had gone to bed she got her chance to thank him.

"It's beautiful, thank you so much. I just hope she is old enough to appreciate what a treasure she has been given."

"It was my pleasure. I enjoyed making it. And don't go putting it away until she's older, I made it for her to play with." With that he walked upstairs before she could say anything else.

Later that night, Sara could hear him prowling around while she lay in bed. She found him back in the locked room drunk, when she went to investigate. She stood in the dark corridor and listened with a heavy heart. He talked to his dead wife as though she could still hear him. 'Can you not accept that she is dead, she is gone from here, gone, gone. Just why are you torturing yourself?' she asked him silently. Only, when at last he staggered back along the corridor safely to his room was she able to go back to bed.

On St. Stephen's morning she found Molly up and dressed and already in the kitchen.

"This is the greatest contraption a body ever had,"

she greeted her, as she wheeled herself around the kitchen in obvious delight. "I put it beside my bed last night, and was able to hoist myself into it this morning." She smiled broadly at Sara, thrilled with her new -found independence. Henry opened the kitchen door when they were eating breakfast.

"Well, what kind of a Christmas did you have?" he asked.

"The best one ever," Molly answered.

"Oh the postman left this down at my place a wheen of days ago. I forgot all about it to this morning," he added handing Sara a tobacco stained crumpled envelope. She just about recognised Maura's writing.

"If you had got this to me before yesterday, it would have made my Christmas. I was that worried at not hearing from her."

He averted his eyes from Sara's guiltily as she spoke. 'God above knows how long he had it in that pocket' Sara thought as she made her way upstairs to read it in private. This was the first correspondence she had from Maura since she sent on her father's letter. Her hands shook as she opened it.

Chapter 10

A New Beginning

Maura folded her father's letter and put it back in the envelope. She knew every word contained in it off by heart, as she had read, and re-read it umpteen times. All her old feelings of hate and resentment of him had vanished, and were replaced with a mixture of pity and love. She knew that she could never forgive him for deporting her like a common criminal. But at least she had a better understanding of his misguided reasons.

She found it hard to imagine him dead. 'You are gone, and I will never see you again,' she told herself in an attempt to make it sink in. But she shed no tears, they just refused to come.

'The house is there for you if you want it' she read over and over. 'I am tempted, God knows I am,' she said aloud to herself. 'But what kind of a future would I have? An unmarried mother alone in a small- minded rural community. I would be little more than an outcast,' she reasoned.

The winter was long and cold, the lack of freedom and exercise made her depressed and morose. The monotony was broken twice a week when Andrew Jefferson and his Mother came to call. She would spend hours getting the nursery spic-and-span. They always spent a happy hour playing with David and taking tea, it was the only time the nursery resounded to the sound of happy laughter.

Ethel Hanley's morning visits were a time of extreme trial in Maura's day. Tight lipped and suspicious her daily barrage of criticism, and hate poured from her mouth like a snake's venom. Maura learned that by appearing to show no emotion, she ran out of steam much quicker. But it was only pretence on Maura's part. The daily ordeal was taking its toll on her self -esteem, and her courage to withstand it was slowly ebbing away.

David had grown and thrived during the two and a half years since she became his nanny. He was an adorable child with a gentle nature. His mother visited him only twice in all that time. On both occasions she showed little interest in her son, no cuddles or kisses, only a mild curiosity passed between mother and child. "I'm getting better now, she told Maura. But I'm not ready to come back. And I couldn't risk going through that again. Anyway, I have given him an Heir to his throne," she added. She was very beautiful to look at, but to Maura she seemed cold and vain. On both occasions Maura felt pity for her child, he would have everything that money could buy, but he needed a mother's love. The one consolation as far as Maura was concerned, was the love and affection shown to him by his grandmother.

The sound of the dreaded jangle of keys approaching the nursery brought morning gloom. Ethel stood in the doorway, her narrow eyes surveying the surroundings suspiciously. She marched over to the laundry cupboard and flung the door open.

"The child's clothing is an untidy mess," she screeched, as she tumbled out the neat piles of laundry on to the floor. "Get it tidied up immediately, you useless lazy bitch." She stood with her hands resting on her hips and watched while Maura folded the laundry, and put it back in the cupboard. David came and sat, next to her whimpering in fear, while keeping his eyes glued to her face. "You will be out of here soon. The child's mother is coming home, and she is employing her old nanny to take care of him," she said with great satisfaction. "That will end old Ma Jefferson and her smart ass son poking their nose in where it's not wanted. No more unannounced visits to the nursery when his mother takes over," she added with a sarcastic smirk.

When Maura finished putting the linen back in the cupboard, she watched her walk over to the sink. Then filling a small enamel bowl with water she went over to the neat stacks of linen and tipped the water in equal quantities on each pile. "Now, get them aired at once. You couldn't run a dog kennel let alone a nursery," she said with a high pitched laugh.

It was only then that Maura saw him standing in the open doorway. In two strides he was across the floor. Ethel had her back to him as he grabbed her by the shoulders and swung her around.

"You evil madwoman. What the hell do you think you're doing?" She stared at Andrew Jefferson with a mixture of fear and contempt. "Get your bags packed. I want you out of this house now," he kept his voice firm, while the muscles of his face and neck contorted in anger.

"Just a minute Mr. Jefferson," she began. "You better consult your mother before you start ordering me around." Her eyes narrowed and her lips formed a snarl as she faced him.

"I know all about your little blackmailing trick. You tricked your way into my father's bed. I know all about it," he spat back at her. For a split second she averted her eyes, and her face reddened. But, only for a second

"You don't frighten me Mr. smart ass Jefferson. I am, employed by your brother. He and he alone can fire me," she yelled back.

"You will be out of this house by nightfall. Now get out of my sight before I do something I'll regret," he stormed as he grabbed her shoulder, and ushered her from the room slamming the door behind her.

He sat on the chair by the door with his head in his hands in silence. Then getting to his feet he came over to where Maura was standing by the window. He gently lifted her chin with his hand until their eyes met.

"Maura, dear little Maura, I'm sorry," he said gently with a quiver in his voice. Maura's knees felt shaky and her face burned as she looked up into his blue eyes. She was terrified of making a fool of herself as she struggled to think of something to say.

"It's all right," was all she could think of saying.

"Damn it, it's not all right. That old spawn of evil has been allowed to terrorise you," he bellowed again in anger. "Stay here, just for a few minutes while I telephone David. I'll only be a minute or two," he said again with a smile before he closed the door behind him.

Maura felt strange, she was annoyed with herself for letting him affect her in that way. 'He is only being kind to me because of the way Ethel Hanley is treating me, you stupid fool,' she told herself firmly. A few minutes later he was back as he had promised.

"Get whatever you need packed. We are going to my mother's house in Long Island for a few days," he said.

When they were in the motor car he said, "Are you all right?"

"I'm fine Mr. Jefferson," she answered in a small voice.

"How long has this been going on?"

"Since I came here. But she has got worse of late," she added.

"I'll never understand why you didn't run from that

hell hole long ago," he sighed.

"But thank you for staying, for his sake," he said looking at the child sitting on Maura's knee. Suddenly, he leant over and kissed her on the cheek. Again she could feel her face blush. When she looked at him he was smiling at her with amusement. "Funny, lovely shy little Maura. You are a whole world away from all the stupid, vain gold diggers I have had the misfortune to know," he said, almost as if he were talking to himself.

The house in Long Island had an atmosphere of friendliness about it. From the cheerful staff to the friendly welcome of Mrs. Jefferson, Maura felt she was in another world. When she put the child to bed, a maid knocked at the nursery door. "Mrs. Jefferson said dinner will be served in half an hour downstairs," she said with a warm smile. When she had gone Maura began to feel nervous. 'What will I wear? And I won't know what to say,' she said aloud in panic. Grabbing her only reasonably half-decent, blue dress she ironed it with the nursery iron as carefully as she could. She brushed her hair and pinned it back at the nape of the neck. On the dot of eight o'clock she made her way nervously downstairs.

"How nice you look dear. Blue suits you," she greeted her with a friendly smile.

"Thank you," Maura replied. As they made their way into the dining room Mrs. Jefferson caught Maura's arm.

"Andrew has been telling me all you have had to endure at the hands of that insanely evil woman. I am so sorry. It is all my fault, I should have come clean years ago," she sighed before continuing. "As it is, I am responsible for the misery she has caused you, and the rest of the staff down the years." She put a reassuring arm around Maura's shoulder and led her into the dining room where Andrew was waiting for them. Their easygoing manner soon put Maura at her ease. To her surprise, she felt relaxed and happy in their company.

"It is about time you had a day off dear," Mrs. Jefferson said. "What about tomorrow?" she asked.

"That would be fine, if you're sure you can manage."

"Of course we can manage, you need a bit of time to yourself."

"I will see that the car is available for you at whatever time you want it," Andrew offered.

"That's very good of you. Thank you," Maura said. Maura felt excited at the prospect of seeing Hannah again. She had so much to tell her, so much had happened.

"I have something of importance to tell you Maura," Mrs. Jefferson's voice broke into her thoughts. "I thought it would be better coming from me. My son's wife is well enough to come home it seems," she sighed softly before going on. "Anyway, she has decided to employ her old Nanny to look after David. I am not happy about it at all. But there is nothing I can do. In my opinion you are far more suitable to look after him than some elderly woman long out of practice," again she sighed deeply. "I'm sorry Maura, but I had to tell you." She patted Maura's arm apologetically.

"They want you to stay for a month or so, until the child gets used to her," Andrew said from across the table. "Please say you will...for the child's sake," he said with concern in his tone.

"Of course I'll stay, for as long as I'm needed," Maura said regaining her composure.

That night she lay in bed unable to sleep. The thought of looking for another job frightened her, leaving her feeling insecure all over again. Although Miss Hanley had made life hell for her, she was the devil she knew. And then there was wee David, she knew that leaving him would cause her much grief, for she loved him like her own. She consoled herself with the thought of seeing Hannah the following day and mulling it over with her was sure to help.

True to his word, Andrew Jefferson had left instructions with his driver to be available to take Maura wherever she wanted to go. She gave him the address of Hannah's apartment, and they set off through the busy streets, a world away from the wealthy middle class opulence from where they came.

"What time do you want me to come back for you Miss?" the driver enquired when they arrived.

"About nine o'clock or so."

"Very well Miss. I'll be waiting for you outside. It wouldn't be safe to leave the car in this district, so I'll wait outside here, O.K?" he explained. Maura nodded.

"See you at nine then," she said.

Hannah greeted her with a warm smile of welcome. It was a smile she had come to know well; wide, honest; you and I are pals it said. Hannah was surrounded by her dressmaking work. Material, finished and unfinished dresses, filled every nook and cranny of the apartment.

"I will have to carry on working while we talk," she explained apologetically. "I have so much work to get through before tomorrow. I dare not stop. If I was working for myself, I reckon I would earn a fortune. As it is I do all the hard slog and my employer gets all the money," she explained.

"Have you ever thought about setting up on your own?" Maura asked.

"Aye, I tried to borrow from the bank once, but they turned me down flat; no security to offer them. So that was that. I will just have to slave away, unless I meet a rich man or something. Enough about me. Tell me your news," she asked.

Hannah listened to Maura's news as she worked, nodding here and there when appropriate.

"Don't worry your head about finding work, there is plenty of work. By the way, can you sew?" she suddenly asked.

"A wee bit. My mother taught me, but I'm no

dressmaker if that's what you're asking."

"You don't need to be a dressmaker. Here, hem this!" she said tossing a frock at her.

"I'll try, but you'll probably have to un-pick it when I've finished," Maura said with a laugh.

"If that is half middling at all I can get you a job here if you want it," Hannah said.

"That sounds very tempting. But I don't think my sewing would be good enough."

"Let's have a look." Hannah said taking the frock from her lap.

"That's good enough for me. And anyway you will learn as you go. What a team we will make, eh," she added with a big broad smile.

"All right you're on. I will be here in about a month. And I'll try and get as much practice in as possible in the meantime," Maura said with confidence.

They shook hands on the deal and giggled like school children. As nine o'clock drew near Maura kept watch from the window for her transport.

"Maura, are you falling for this Andrew Jefferson? You have talked about him all afternoon?" Hannah asked suddenly.

"Don't be ridiculous," Maura dismissed her angrily. "He has been kind to me..., well, because I think he feels sorry for me, that's all. Anyhow he is a wealthy man, who has the pick of all the beautiful society woman of New York. Why, Hannah Mc Laughlin sometimes you don't seem to have the sense you were born with," she ended sounding flustered.

"Don't get on your high horse, just wondered that's all," Hannah giggled.

The motor car arrived on the dot of nine. Maura was surprised to find Andrew Jefferson sitting in the back seat, when she got in.

"This was on my way home," he explained. "Did you have a good day?" he enquired.

"Yes, very good. And thank you for the use of the car Mr. Jefferson," she said.

"Think nothing of it. My pleasure."

"Hannah thinks I might get a job as a dressmaker with her, if her employer agrees," she said.

"Who does your friend work for?" he asked.

"Her name is Wentworth. She owns a fashion store. Hannah makes most of the outfits for her customers, she works from the apartment, designing and making the clothes."

"I see. Your friend does all the work and her employer makes all the money, eh," he said. She laughed.

"Funny, that's just what Hannah said."

He leant across the seat and looked at her closely, before asking.

"I hope you weren't thinking about working from that apartment?"

"I wàs, why?" she asked, looking puzzled.

"Because it's not a very safe neighbourhood."

"Hannah did say she would like to move when finances permit. She wanted to start her own fashion business. But the bank wouldn't lend her the money. She had no security to offer them, you see." Andrew nodded thoughtfully.

Maura returned to David Jefferson's home with a mixture of relief and sadness. Ethel Hanley was gone. She could walk around the house freely at last, without fear of the dreaded figure, descending on her from a hidden doorway or dark corridor. The mornings brought no fear of the sound of keys clicking together, as she waited in fear of her evil tongue. But she dreaded the day when she would have to leave the place that had become her home. Her heart sank every time she thought about leaving the child that she had grown to love so dearly. She wondered what his new nanny would be like. She half made up her mind not to like her.

It was decided that the new nanny would come two weeks before Maura was due to leave, so that David would get to know her before Maura's departure.

Miss Donnelly was a large jolly woman in late middle age, who, had a genuine love for children, much to Maura's relief. David liked her almost immediately, and soon referred to her as 'Nanna Don.' This eased the pain of Maura's impending departure, a little.

"You have no need to worry about him you know, I will give him all the affection he needs," Miss Donnelly said reassuringly." And you can come to see him as often as you wish," she added with a motherly smile.

"Thank you," Maura said tearfully, as the older woman put a reassuring hand on her shoulders. "The poor mite won't get a lot of affection from his mother, but he will get all the love from me that I can give," she said with conviction.

Andrew Jefferson and his mother made their usual twice-weekly visits much to everyone's delight. Watching Andrew as he played with David, Maura felt a painful pang of grief come over her. 'I will miss him too. I like him. I like his arrogant blue eyes, and the entirely different look that comes into them when he gazes at the child. I will miss him a lot, an awful lot,' she had to confess to herself, while struggling to keep her emotions hidden.

"I have something to discuss with you," he said as he was leaving. "I will pick you up at around two o'clock tomorrow," he added with a serious note in his voice, that left Maura puzzled for the entire evening. They sat facing each other in the tearoom the following afternoon. "I have been thinking about what you said about your friend and the fashion business," he began. "Well, I have a proposition to put to you. I am willing to finance you both, to enable you to start your own business. A three way partnership."

"But, but....we couldn't let you risk your money," Maura stammered. "What if it went wrong?"

"I don't think it will go wrong. If I didn't believe it was a sound investment I wouldn't suggest it. And anyway I owe you something," he said with a soft smile.

"I can't wait to tell Hannah; it will be her dream come true," Maura said breathlessly, suddenly feeling elated.

"No time like the present; come, the chauffeur will have us there in a jiffy. And anyway I want to meet this friend of yours....if we are to be partners."

They found Hannah surrounded by dresses and material. She became flustered by her unexpected guests, and began frantically to clear a space for Andrew to sit down.

"Oh, Hannah I have great news; the most wonderful news. You are going to have your own fashion business; we are to be partners," Maura shouted excitedly, while Hannah looked at her open mouthed.
Andrew sat silently watching them, smiling to himself in obvious amusement. When Maura finished explaining the plan to her, Hannah asked.

"Are you sure you want to risk your money Mr. Jefferson?"

"I'm no expert on ladies fashion; but the work you have done looks pretty good to me," he said looking at the numerous outfits hanging around the room.

"I am a good dressmaker; but I know nothing about running a business," she said with a frown.

"No need to concern yourself about that end of it.

There are people we can pay, who will look after that part of it; until you both get the hang of it."

"I am very much indebted to you; in fact I am so excited I could scream," she said with a giggle. On an impulse she ran over and kissed him on the cheek.

"I think this calls for a small celebration. I will book a table at Marty's. I will be back in an hour or so; Okay?" he asked.

"Thank you, that would be grand," Hannah said, unable to contain the excitement in her voice.
When he had gone the two friends danced around the room in happy excitement.

"God bless Andrew Jefferson; I can't believe my good fortune," Hannah said as she waltzed around the small room with a dressmaker's dummy clothed in an evening gown. "We better find something suitable to wear; after all we must look like fashion designers," Hannah said searching through the dresses heaped around the room. She selected a dark blue chiffon dress for Maura. "This should suit you nicely. Go on try it on," she urged. "It's one that I made for a customer last year; she never came back to collect it. If I didn't know different I would swear I had made it especially for you," Hannah said as Maura made her appearance wearing the dress.

"You look stunning in it; just perfect."

"Are you sure it's not a bit...,well too grand for me?"

"No it's not in the least too grand for you. Oh, ye of

little faith," she said with a shake of her head.

"Are you sure I don't look silly?" Maura asked again.

"For the last time, listen to me...you look lovely—right?"

"I believe you then," Maura smiled, suddenly feeling light hearted.

When Andrew arrived to pick them up both, were ready and waiting for him. He stood in the doorway and gave a low whistle.

"You look wonderful; both of you. Come, your chariot awaits," he said as they linked arms and went towards the car.

In Marty's a waiter escorted them to their table where a bottle of champagne sat cooling in an ice bucket.

"To our partnership," Andrew boomed as they clicked their glasses together with laughter.

"Now; have you decided what you are going to name your fashion business?" he asked.

"No, we haven't got that far yet. Have you any ideas Mr. Jefferson?"

Let me see. What is your surname again?"

"Mc Laughlin."

"How about Laughlin-Quinn; or Quinn-Laughlin?" he suggested.

"I think Quinn-Laughlin sounds better," Hannah said. "What do you think Maura?" he asked.

"That sounds fine to me. But I think we should

include your name; after all you are financing it."

"No need. I am the silent partner. So raise your glasses to the birth of Quinn-Laughlin."

It was midnight by the time they dropped Hannah off at her apartment.

"I like Hannah; she's a nice girl, and what's more she's ambitious. The new business will go far, if I'm any judge." he said leaning back on the seat.

"I really enjoyed tonight. And it was the first time I ever tasted champagne. Thank you again Mr. Jefferson."

"Andrew, call me Andrew; for heavens sake."

"All right; thank you Andrew."

"That's better, partner," he said.

She felt safe and contented as the car travelled through the quiet streets. 'I wish I could stay here forever feeling the safe comfort of his nearness,' she thought contentedly.

Two weeks later she made her sad farewells to her charge and his new nanny. She promised to visit as often as she could. At the bottom of the stairs David Jefferson senior waited for her. "I just want to say thank you for all you have done for my son. "I'm sorry if I have been negligent. Well here is your reference, and a token of my appreciation," he said handing her two envelopes. Opening the first envelope in the car, she was amazed to find it contained two hundred dollars.

The new apartment was in a leafy suburb, and was airy and

spacious. Hannah was in high spirits, delighted with her new surroundings and had already started making model outfits for display.

"I have just come back from viewing our new fashion store," Hannah greeted her with a grin of pleasure. "Quinn-Laughlin, Quin-Laughlin," she repeated triumphantly, we are going to become famous Maura."

"I hope so Hannah for your sake. But I wish you had a more experienced partner than me."

"You'll soon learn. Just wait and see, in a few months time you will know all there is to know about fashion."

"I hope you're right." Maura said, trying to sound more confident than she felt.

In the early weeks business was slow and customers few and far between, then slowly but surely they had more orders than they could cope with. It meant working late into the night to meet the demands of the stream of fashion conscious society women who honoured them with their custom.

"Congratulations to you both," Andrew Jefferson boomed from the hallway when Hannah answered the door one evening. His big frame loomed above Maura as she sewed the last of the tiny pearl buttons on the bodice of an evening gown.

"It is exactly a year since the birth of Quinn Laughlin. And you are already showing a sizeable profit.

Come we must go out and celebrate."

"Sorry, I can't Mr. Jefferson. I have an urgent order to complete." But Maura can go with you," Hannah suggested.

"I don't like the idea of you both slaving away in the evenings like this. You can afford to hire some extra help from now on."

"That would make a big difference to our workload," Hannah said with a nod of her head and a broad grin.

As she stepped out of the car Maura saw him standing on the pavement, only the side of his face was visible to her. But it was enough to bring a terrible fear to her heart. She could feel her whole body tremble uncontrollably. She was a helpless child again coming from school, she saw his evil grin, smelled his sweat, heard his threats and felt the terror. As she stood paralysed with fear, the man turned around, the front of his face bore no resemblance to Seamus.

"Maura, Maura, what's wrong? You look as if you've seen a ghost." Andrew's voice seemed to come from a great distance.

"I....thought...I saw someone I once knew," she stammered.

"Whoever it was you thought you saw, was no friend by the look of you." With an arm around her shoulder he steadied her gently to a corner table of the restaurant. Seated opposite Andrew Jefferson, Maura felt uncomfortable under his gaze. "Maura," he said softly. "What is troubling you? There is something." He could feel her hands stiffen under his as he spoke. Her voice quivered as she answered his urgent question.

"I was once frightened.... by a man I knew as a child. And I mistakenly thought I saw him on the pavement."

"He must have terrified you from the way you are shaking."

"It was nothing....really. Just me being silly." The look on his face told her that he didn't believe her attempts to brush the incident off lightly. He gently squeezed her trembling hands without comment.

When the waiter brought the menu, Maura asked. "Would you mind if I just had coffee? I'm not hungry."

"Of course I don't mind. Would you like to go back to my apartment? We can have coffee there and see my abode at the same time."

Maura nodded. She wanted to get away from the crowded restaurant.

Andrew Jefferson's apartment looked just as Maura imagined it would, there was a cosy practicality about the place, that made her feel more at ease. He placed the coffee on the table, and sat down in the big leather chair opposite her. As she looked at his kind face and smiling eyes, she felt a lovely sense of peace sweeping over her. She had to admit the truth that she had tried to deny even to herself. She had fallen in love with this giant of a man, almost from the first day, when he walked into the nursery. And she knew that it was a love that could never be anything more than a hopeless dream; a hopeless love, that could never be known to anyone but herself.

"Maura I have something important to ask you," he said softly. "Then you can tell me what frightened you." Then taking her hands in his, he said. "I have become very fond of you Maura. In fact, more than fond of you. But I can't seem to get really close to you. For example, that episode earlier, with the man on the pavement. You didn't tell me the truth, did you?" She could feel the blood rush to her face. "I suppose I have no right to pry. But I love you. I have loved you from the first day I met you." Then leaning over, he knelt in front of her and kissed her softly on the lips.

Maura felt her knees turn to jelly, she could feel her whole being, melt towards him with a joy such as she had never felt before. Then almost as suddenly her joy was replaced by a feeling of hopelessness. 'I can't tell him the truth; not yet. Oh God above, what am I going to do?' She wanted more than anything else, to spend the rest of her life with this man, she loved him more than life itself. 'If only I could block out the past, pretend it never happened.' She knew that sooner or later she would have to tell him the truth. But for now she could see no further into the future, than she could see along the dark wet streets outside.

"Will you marry me?"

His question sent her emotions into a frenzy, which went

from joy to despair as she sat motionless. "Well...I hope I haven't frightened you away." His whole face became suffused with hope and happiness.

"This is so sudden," she said softly, while inside her heart was breaking. 'God, Oh God, must I be punished forever because of the past?'

Touching her cheek gently, he said "It's all right Maura, I think I might be frightening you away. But I will live in hope that you will in time learn to love me."

"I..I think you are the nicest man I have ever met," she whispered.

"Now tell me what frightened you earlier?" he asked again.

"It was just....someone, someone that looked like a man who I was afraid of as a child, that's all," she stammered.

"It was most unlikely that the man you saw, was the same man who you knew as a child. If you will allow me, I promise that nothing or no one will ever frighten you again," he said quietly.

"But Andrew, Why me? You could have the pick of all the rich and beautiful women in New York...In all America."

"The answer is simple. I love you."

She looked down at the big gentle hands that held hers, and felt that her heart would break. Part of her wanted to blurt out the reasons why their love could never be anything more than a beautiful dream. But she just couldn't; not just yet.

"Andrew, would you wait for an answer. You see I want to go home to Ireland for a few weeks to see my Mother." When she had spoken the words she could scarcely believe what she had just said. It was almost as if someone else had spoken for her. Then she heard him say.

"I will wait. How ever long it takes, I will wait."

The remainder of the evening went by in a haze. Maura tried to block out the feelings of panic that seized her periodically. Most of the time passed in a dreamy haze as if she were hypnotised in a magic spell. Only after they had kissed each other goodnight, and she walked up the stairs to the apartment did the magic bubble burst in her head.

When she opened the door of the apartment she found it in darkness. A glimmer of light shone from under Hannah's door. Going over to the door she was about to knock, but then thought better of it; instead she sat on the couch in the darkness and let the tears fall silently down her face.

Dawn's early light showing dimly through the window reminded her that the night hours had passed.

"Have you been out all night?" Hannah asked, looking down at her. Maura jumped.

"You gave me a start. I didn't hear you get up,"

"Well, where you out all night?" she asked again.

Maura shook her head slowly.

"Good God, you look awful. What's wrong?" She stared into space without answering her. "Is it Andrew Jefferson? Did he do something to you?" She slowly lifted her gaze to meet Hannah's.

"No Hannah, he did nothing to me. It's more a case of what I did to myself." Hannah looked puzzled.

"I'll get you a strong cup of coffee and you can tell me what this is all about," she said as she went to the kitchen.

Over coffee Maura told her friend about the events of the night before. Hannah remained silent until Maura had finished.

"I have known for a good while that he was falling for you. Only you can decide if his love is strong enough to face the truth about your past. Just remember Maura, that nothing of what happened to you was your fault. And I for one don't think that you should have to suffer for all time because of it," Hannah breathed heavily as she searched for the right words. Then she asked. "Why did you tell him you were going home to Ireland?" Maura stared vacantly ahead shaking her head before she answered.

"To be honest Hannah, I don't know why I told him that. I suppose I was just playing for time. I just couldn't tell him that how ever, much I love him, I couldn't let him waste his life on me. I just want to live in this beautiful make believe world for a wee while longer."

"Maybe going back home for a while wouldn't be

such a bad idea. It might just help you to get your thoughts straight."

Maura's face lit up for a moment, but soon became sombre again, then she said. "I would only be running away. And anyway I couldn't leave you high and dry, we have a business to run."

"I could manage on my own for a couple of months. But Maura, Andrew Jefferson is not the kind of man who will run away from you because of your past; a past that was no fault of your own."

"Hannah, how could you believe that? How could I expect him to throw his life away on the likes of me? A woman who was repeatedly raped by her relative; had an child out of wedlock, deported by her own father, and tried to commit suicide. How understanding can a man be?" she asked sadly. "I can't tell you what to do Maura. But whatever you decide to do I will help in any way I can. Now I must go and open the store." When she reached the door she looked back at Maura, it hurt her to see the pained expression in her eyes. With a sigh she shut the door and left her alone.

Alone again Maura made the decision to return to Ireland. 'I could become his mistress, without having to tell him anything,' she said aloud to herself. But quickly following on came, the sobering reality of her life as Andrew Jefferson's mistress. She knew in her heart that he would one day want to find a suitable wife and mother for his children, someone like the beautiful young woman who had accompanied him to the theatre, on the night he had provided tickets for Hannah and herself. It was still painful to remember how she had felt on seeing them together, when she smiled falsely to hide the jealous ache in her heart.

By the afternoon she had firmly made up her mind to return home for good.

She wrote a long letter to her mother, in which she poured out her heart, ending with her decision to return.

In the days that followed she busied herself with the business, and booking her passage, and for most of the time she could dispel the shadows.

Sitting in the back of Andrew's car, her hand tightly clasped in his, she thought about how strange it was to think that her return home was to be steeped in the same sad parting as had been her lot when leaving Ireland.

"I will count the hours until your return," he said quietly. "Just remember I love you. And I expect you to write every day."

Maura looked deeply into his eyes and nodded. When they reached the dock he bent down and kissed her gently on the lips. "God speed! And hurry back my darling," he said softly.

Once again the lump in her throat made speech impossible, she nodded, then placing a kiss on his big gentle hand she climbed on board the ship almost blinded by her tears.

As the ship slowly made its way out of the harbour she watched as Andrew's big frame slowly grew smaller until his face just became a blur. She followed the steward up the wide stairway to the first class cabin. As she stepped inside, she saw the red roses. Then opening the small white envelope she read;

"I will always love you, and I will count the hours until you are back home with me. ANDREW". Throwing herself on the bed she sobbed until exhaustion sent her to sleep.

Chapter 11

The Reunion

Sara read, and re-read Maura's letter.

'Poor, poor wee Maura, must your whole life be ruined for ever more because of what an evil man did?' she whispered to the empty kitchen.

She missed Molly now more than ever. This would be the first letter from Maura that she had not read aloud to her. It was just three weeks since she found her dead in bed. At first she had thought she was asleep. She was lying on her right side with her eyes closed, the position she always found her in when she brought her morning tea. It was only when she didn't reply to her morning greeting that she knew that something was wrong.

As Sara looked around the kitchen, everything reminded her of her old friend. Mary Kate found it impossible to understand that she would not see Molly again. She looked for her in every nook of the kitchen each morning before asking,

"Where, Molly?" Sara had done her best to explain

what death meant, and that Molly wouldn't be coming back, but she was just too young to accept the finality of death. James Thompson had taken the death of Molly very badly. He was consumed with sorrow and guilt, and hid himself away in the study with the bottle. He suddenly emerged sober one morning as Sara was putting Mollys' few belongings in an old trunk. He stood silently in the doorway watching her for a few minutes before he spoke.

"She had very few belongings to leave behind her. Not much to show for a lifetimes work and loyalty," he added with a sigh.

Still kneeling, Sara looked at his troubled face for a few seconds before answering,

"Molly may not have had many possessions, but that didn't make her life a failure."

"Maybe not, but she deserved better than she got from me," he said eyeing her pensively.

"She didn't see it that way. She was very fond of you. Aye, even when you disappeared that time, she insisted that it wasn't deliberate, And she was right." she said looking him straight in the eye.

"Sara, Sara, there you go again, trying to find good where there is none."

He walked over to the window, and stood vacantly staring out with a grim expression on his face. Getting up from her kneeling position Sara walked over to join him.

"Molly was happy here for most of her life. She had a bad time I grant it, but sure we all have bad times. And she had a long life, and died peacefully in her own bed. And she saw a lot of good in you. If it wasn't for the cursed drink he, would be a grand man, she used to say. And she was right."

He turned to look at her. She saw a hint of a smile on his face, before he answered.

"Why have I had the good fortune to be surrounded by women who are determined to see good in a drunken waster like me?" he asked, with a shake of his head.

"Maybe it is because we are able to see you in a way that you refuse to see yourself."

"Correction. In a way I'm not able to see myself" he sighed.

"Mr. Thompson."

"James."

"James I need to talk to you about a letter I got from Maura. She is coming home."

"Well, that must be good news for you," he said.

"I can't wait to see her again. But it's her reasons for coming home that's bothering me."

She looked away from him and out the window with a sad expression for a few seconds before she spoke to him again.

"She fell in love with the brother of her former employer, and he asked her to marry him. But he knows nothing about Mary Kate, or about her past. And she can't tell him," she said sadly.

"So she is running away."

"Aye, that is about the height of it," Sara concluded.

"Do you know Sara, most of my life is spent in a dark place that I am unable to escape from. But when I see Mary Kate and listen to her happy giggles I feel a stirring of joy. If she were to leave this house..." His voice trailed off, and his eyes held a deep sadness. Then he said.

"I suppose I am being selfish. After all Maura is her mother. But if she takes her away from us..?"

"I dare not even think about that," Sara said, with a shudder in her voice. "I hope she doesn't want to go back to Clougher. I couldn't face going back to that house, with all it's memories. And anyway I don't want to leave here," she added.

"Sara if you were ever to leave us, I don't know what we would do." He walked towards the door and stood for a while with his hand on the knob.

"Mary Kate can read a little already. She's such a bright little thing," he suddenly said, turning to face Sara with a smile of pleasure.

"Tell Maura that she has a home here with us if she wishes." He closed the door behind him and was gone, before she had time to answer.

She sat staring at the door he had just closed lost in thought. Maura's return brought feeling of joy and fear. Now that James had offered her a home here, it eased her fears about losing Mary Kate a little. 'But, what if she didn't want a home here?' she asked herself. She sat down on Molly's old trunk with a heavy heart. 'What would your advice have been Molly?' she asked aloud. She found it a strange irony that she should fear the return of her beloved daughter. She had missed her so much during the past three years, and now she was afraid; afraid to share Mary Kate. Getting up she decided to talk her fears over with Jean, she could hear her in the kitchen talking to Mary Kate. In spite of her age and increasing frailty, she had taken over Molly's cooking jobs in the kitchen. When she opened the kitchen door, she stood for a moment and watched her getting Mary Kate's breakfast ready; talking to her as she worked. Jean had often told her that Mary Kate gave her a reason to get up in the morning. As she watched them, Sara felt a surge of pleasure sweep over her, as she again marvelled at how this small being had won the hearts of everyone she had come into contact with.

Jean carefully folded Maura's letter, then she raised her eyes to meet Sara's before she spoke.

"Poor child she must be heartbroken about leaving the man she loves. I think she's a fool mind you, because if he is really genuine I know he would understand."

"But, you have to admit that it is a lot for any man to understand," Sara said, quietly.

"Maybe, but I would have to risk it if it were me. I would have to know what he is made of. But, this is all for another day, we must concentrate now on getting ready for her arrival," she said briskly.

Sara held Mary Kate's hand nervously as the train pulled

into the station. She stared at the alighting passengers in turn. Then she saw her step down from the train. She saw a sophisticated, lovely young woman; gone was the child that she had said goodbye to just three and a half years ago. Then Maura saw them, and walked slowly towards them. Letting go of Mary Kate's hand, Sara held out her arms. She ran the last few yards and into her mother's arms, laughing and crying almost at the one time. Then she turned to Mary Kate and lifted her into her arms. As she tried to hug her she turned her head towards Sara with her chubby arms outstretched.

"Nana, Nana," she cried.

"Give her time," Sara said softly, taking Mary Kate out of her arms.

The pony ride home was mostly spent in silence. As they reached the driveway Maura asked anxiously.

"Are you sure these people will want me intruding on them?"

"They are as excited as I am about your arrival. Have no fears on that score," Sara answered with a smile. As the pony trotted along the avenue, the evening sun shone red and gold, casting it's rays on the water below.

"How lovely it all is. I had almost forgotten, Maura said with a sigh.

Jean stood in the hall door when they reached it.

"Welcome home," she said to Maura with a warm smile.

"Come into the drawing room. Tea is ready."

Maura sat down on the big couch close to the blazing fire.

"This is a lovely room," she said.

"We have your mother to thank for that. She rescued it from damp and the neglect of years." Maura's attention was diverted from Jean when she saw Mary Kate's little face watching her warily from the door. She found herself searching her features for any resemblance of Seamus. And to her great relief she found none. She smiled at her encouragingly, but she stared back at her solemnly.

"She will need a bit of time to get to know you," Jean said quietly.

Just as she was finishing her tea James Thompson came in.

"Welcome Maura," he boomed. "If I met you in the street I would know who you were. You look so much like your mother. And Mary Kate here," he added as he lifted her high in the air. Maura watched as Mary Kate giggled with delight, and she couldn't help feeling envious. Both of these people were strangers to her, in spite of their obvious attempts to make her welcome.

These dark thoughts made her feel ungrateful especially when later, she saw the trouble Jean had taken to get her room ready. A bright fire blazed in the grate, and snowy white lace curtains hung at the big window overlooking the sea. She thanked the old woman kindly.

"So long as you'll be happy here dear, it was my great pleasure," she said with a gentle smile.

"Did my mother tell you about the reason for my return home?" she suddenly asked Jean.

"Yes Maura she told me. Your mother and I are great friends. We share most things."

"I see." Maura said tensely, shifting her gaze from Jean and out the window into the gathering darkness.

"I hope you are not angry with her Maura. She loves you very dearly, and I am the only one she can confide in."

"I'm not angry. I am just not used to strangers knowing all about my personal business."

Jean sighed deeply before she answered.

"Oh, dear. And I so wanted us to get off on a good footing."

"I'm sorry, I didn't mean to offend you. I'm just a bit jealous I suppose. You are both strangers, and I see how much you mean to my mother and my child....how much more at ease they are in your company than mine," she said, looking back at Jean.

Going over to the window Jean put her arms around her.

"I understand just how you feel. But please, give us time."

Maura felt all the tension, leave her, as she warmed to the gentle affection of Jean Thompson.

Maura's days at the rectory passed slowly. Mary Kate warmed to her gradually. They walked to the shore on dry days hand in hand, and this gave Maura some comfort. She tried not to think of Andrew, but in spite of her best efforts he was constantly in her thoughts. She read his letter at least twice a day, and she had answered it more than once a day, only to tear it up again.

164

The May sun shone warm as they climbed the path from the shore.

"I'm tired," Mary Kate wailed.

"We'll sit here and rest a while," Maura said.

James Thompson suddenly appeared from behind the hill. Mary Kate's face lit up with joy as she ran to greet him.

"Hello, wee lady," he said cheerfully, lifting her into his arms. "I've got something for you." Reaching into his pocket he produced a small book. "It's not easy to get books for this age group," he commented. Then he sat down on a rock close to Maura.

"You are very good to her," Maura said.

"She is very good for me. Gives me something to think about besides myself." He looked deeply into Maura's face in silence, then he said.

"You are not happy, are you?"

Looking away from his gaze she stared at the shore below, and without looking at him she said.

"You are right, I'm not as happy as I should be."

"Would you tell me why?" She sighed deeply before she asked.

"How much did my mother tell you?"

"On the night she arrived here with the child, she told me a bit about the circumstances surrounding her birth."

"Did she tell you anything about my life in America, or why I came home?"

"Only the briefest details. I'm a good listener," he

added arching his brows. Looking away to hide the sudden unwanted tears that sprang into her eyes, she said,

"If only I could rid myself of the past, then maybe I would have a future."

"I'm afraid you will have to enlighten me a bit more," he said quietly.

"I fell in love with a wonderful man called Andrew Jefferson. I didn't think for a minute that he would return that love. But he did," she nervously twisted her hankie around her fingers as she spoke.

"As you probably already know the awful secrets of my past, I don't need to tell you that I couldn't rely them to the man I love."

"Why do you have to tell him anything? Surely he loves you as you are.

Because it wouldn't be honest if I didn't tell him," she answered, her sad eyes begging his understanding.

"Maura, when it comes to advice, I am the last person on earth to offer it. As you probably know, I try to escape my own regrets in a bottle. So, I can only advise you on how to avoid ending up like me," his intense eyes made her feel uncomfortable.

"Well, what advice would you give me then? And don't expect me to be less than honest by keeping my past a secret."

"Well, in that case, tell him the truth, write to him. Or, go back to New York and tell him face to face. But, don't spend the rest of your life wondering."

"Is that it?" she asked.

"Yes, that's it. He lent across the space between then, taking her hand in his he said.

"Maura please don't take Mary Kate away from us. She gives us all a reason to live." Looking away from him she said sharply.

"She is my child. She's all I've got left."

"I know, I know. Forgive me. I should have kept my thoughts to myself." Getting to his feet, he looked down at her again. "Think a little about what I said."
She nodded briefly as he went.

Chapter 12

Dispelling Ghosts

Sara sighed deeply as she stood at the sink preparing the vegetables for lunch. The rain coming down in torrents almost blocking out the light, seemed to add further to her depression. Maura's obvious unhappiness had cast a shadow of gloom over the house, she seemed to walk around in a gloomy trance, and even Mary Kate's happy chatter failed to bring a glimmer of joy to her face. At times Sara felt anger bubbling to the surface, she felt like shouting at her.

'What right has she to bring more sadness into our lives? Haven't we suffered enough?'

Jean's voice coming suddenly from the doorway interrupted her thoughts.

"Do you need any help?" she asked.

"I've nearly finished. But thanks for offering."

"What's wrong Sara? You seem so preoccupied these days. Come, sit down for a minute and talk to me. Is it Maura?" Sara nodded and sat down at the big table facing Jean.

"She seems so unhappy and sad. And I feel guilty and angry, all at the same time. I feel that I should have protected her from that evil man who ruined her whole life." Jean bent over and touched her hand.

"Sara how could you have known what was going on? None of it was your fault; none of it," she repeated with a sharp tone in her voice.

"I wish I truly believed that Jean. She has changed so much that, there are times when I wonder if she is the same girl that I reared." She stared out the window in silence for a few minutes before she asked,

"Jean, if I only knew what I could do or say to make her happy again."

"She has fallen in love Sara. She has run away from the man she loves rather than tell, him the truth about her past. She is afraid of rejection poor child."

Sara looking grimly at Jean said, "for the first time in ages I felt content, almost happy. But this has cast a shadow of sorrow over my life once again. I suppose I was never destined to be happy."

"Nonsense Sara. You of all people have a right to be happy. You are the most caring and capable human being I have ever known. This will work out somehow, you'll see."

"I hope you're right, I really do. Because I have a terrible fear that she will take off one of these days taking Mary Kate with her. She can't wander around here like a lost unhappy soul for the rest of her days."

"It won't come to that Sara, between us we will think of some way out of this dilemma. I'll talk to her again and see what we can come up with."

Her eyes held a look of concern that brought gratitude to Sara's heart for her good fortune in finding a friend like Jean. When later that day Maura told her that she intended to go to Clougher the following morning her fears were renewed.

"Do you want me to go with you love?"

"Thanks for offering, but this is something I must do alone," Maura said walking swiftly out of the room before Sara could ask any more questions, and she knew that she was in for another anxious day.

The following afternoon Maura made her way slowly up the brae towards her old home in Clougher. Suddenly the house came into view, and she stood as if in a trance staring at the house that had been her home. The dilapidated appearance shocked her, even though her mother had warned her about it's derelict state before she left. When she reached the door she fumbled in her pocket for the key with shaking hands. The key turned in the lock with surprising ease, and she walked inside and looked around the damp smelling kitchen for the first time in four years. As her eyes adjusted to the dimness, she saw the old gun in the corner. Walking over to it she stroked it with her gloved hand, as every word in her fathers letter came back to her. Sitting down on a dusty chair she tried to control her shaking limbs. Maybe, her mother had been right when she said that she shouldn't come. Getting up she walked over to the window and stared out through the swaying cobwebs at the fields, and onwards between the hills to the blue grey sea. From the doorway she glanced again at the kitchen, then with a sigh she went out into the warm sunshine. Locking the door she walked on up the lane. When she reached the garden gate of Seamus' house she felt the old awful fear returning; she could hear her heart thundering in her ears. When she had regained some of her composure she walked through the gateway and up to the door. As she stared at the rotting door, she drew back on her heels almost paralysed by fear. She lifted the latch and to her astonishment it creaked open. Stepping warily inside she looked around the dirty damp kitchen and shook uncontrollable at the mere memory of him. Suddenly she was seized by a terrible burning, explosive anger.

"Damn you to hell you evil bastard," she shouted at the emptiness.

"Damn you. Damn you. Damn you," she repeatedly shouted.

Suddenly sobs shook her whole body, as the pent up hate and anger seemed to explode inside her head. Stumbling outside she picked up a large piece of rock and hurdled, it at the window. She gathered stones from the ground and continued to throw them at the windows, all the while shouting obscenities until she was finally exhausted.

She sat on the wall until her sobs ceased. She felt a strange calmness sweep over her as she sat looking at the broken glass glinting eerily in the glow of the setting sun. Walking slowly towards the rectory gates she thought about Andrew for the umpteenth time. She wondered what he was doing right now, her love for him came in painful bursts of regret. It was a fine night with a silver moon that came and went amid slowly drifting clouds. Just beyond the gates she heard her Mothers voice.

"Is that you Maura? Are you all right?" she asked. As she came up to her, she held out her arms. "I was so worried about you," she said, as they hugged each other.

"I'm all right. It helped me to go back and face up to my fear," Maura answered as they linked arms and walked towards the big grey house that looked more inviting silhouetted by the silvery light.

Chapter 13

Secrets

Sara felt hurt about being kept in the dark about James Thompson's sudden departure to visit a sick relative.

"He will be away for six or seven weeks," Jean had explained as they packed his trunk. Sara felt hurt about his not telling her himself. Something about Jean's attitude made her suspicious; she felt that she was hiding something from her.

The steady rhythm of the pony's trotting hooves lulled Sara into a trance like state. James Thompson sat silently opposite her, the reins held loosely in his hands, and his eyes staring straight ahead. He had made no attempt to explain his sudden departure to her, and she felt a strange ache of hurt at his silence.

When they reached the station he turned the pony around and went to find the porter. As the porter wheeled his trunk on to the platform, he turned to Sara as she stood at the pony's head. With a strange sad expression on his face he took her hand in his.

"Wish me luck Sara," he said quietly. Then he bent his head and kissed her gently on the cheek and was gone. She stood staring at the station entrance, with the feel of his lips still warm on her cheek, "God go with you," she whispered. She felt mystified at his strange behaviour, and again felt hurt about being kept in the dark. When she had unyoked the pony, she went into the kitchen.

"I have the kettle boiled," Jean greeted her.

"Maura and Mary Kate have gone to the shore." Sara put her tea -cup down and looked across at Jean.

"Why has James gone? I get the feeling that you are keeping me in the dark," she added with a look of hurt. Jean looked away avoiding her eyes as she spoke.

"I can't tell you Sara. But it will all become clear to you later, I promise," with a look that pleaded for her understanding. Then she said, "please don't ask me again."

Sara shugged her shoulders and was silent.

Sara climbed the stairs, when she reached the landing she walked slowly towards the nursery. She stopped at the door of the study, then on an impulse she opened the door and went in. It all seemed so silent and lonely. Going over to the desk she quickly sorted through the letters, but there was nothing to give her any clues about his sudden departure. Sighing deeply she went over to the window and looked out. She was suddenly, overwhelmed by a feeling of loneliness. 'I miss him,' she said to herself.

This feeling surprised her and left her feeling strangely bewildered. From the doorway she looked back into the room, and again felt the stab of loneliness. She closed the door quietly and went back towards her room. On passing the locked room she had a sudden compelling urge to go in. She turned the handle and much to her surprise the door squeaked open. The room still had the same smell of lavender, and again she experienced the calming peaceful atmosphere that she remembered. She stood in front of the painting of the beautiful young woman, and wondered why her image continually hung around in her thoughts like the mist in the valley on a summer morning. Going over to the window she pulled back one of the heavy velvet curtains and looked out. She watched as Maura and Mary Kate made their way up the path towards the house. A broad smile crossed her face as she watched Mary Kate's curls bounce as she skipped on ahead of her mother. As she watched she was overwhelmed with maternal feelings of love for them. Once again she shivered as she again faced the possibility of Maura taking Mary Kate away from her. She closed the door of the room and ran hastily downstairs just in time to greet them in the hall.

"Nana, look I got shells," she said as she ran into her arms.

"They are lovely sweetheart," Sara said happily as she buried her face in her soft downy curls. Looking up at Maura she sensed resentment in her eyes, with a quick smile she hid the feeling of fear that shot through her.

Sara carried the tray of tea into the drawing room. Jean was slumped in the leather chair by the fire, her knitting dangling down from her lap. Putting the tray down, Sara said in a loud voice, "I've brought your tea." She woke up and rubbed her eyes.

"I must have dozed off., old age I expect," she said with a yawn.

"I'm going to start spring cleaning tomorrow. If nothing else it will keep my mind away from other things," Sara announced, handing her a cup of tea.

"I'll help in any way I can. But I'm not a lot of use for any heavy work anymore. I miss looking after Mary Kate you know. But I suppose it's good for her to get out in the fresh air. Do you know Sara she can read quite a bit. I went over her wee books with her that James made, and even when I covered the drawings with my hand, she knew most of the words. She is so clever," she added ,with an indulgent smile. Sara was silent for a while before she said,

"I'm amazed at the trouble James went to in making books for her. I had no idea that he could draw like that. I never would have dreamt that first night when I came here in desperation, that he would have taken to her like he has." Then turning to Jean she said, "she keeps asking where he is. But then I'm no wiser than she is."

"I know, I know Sara. But I still can't tell you, please believe me."

She gave Sara that look that said don't ask again. During

the following days Sara absorbed herself totally in the spring- cleaning. And at night she was left with just enough energy to crawl into bed. She was pleased that Maura seemed a little less strained than she had been. But when she thought about her future the fear that lay just below the surface came back to haunt her. She missed Mary Kate at bedtime far more than she dared to admit. Maura had of late taken her to sleep in her room, but she always seemed to make her way back to Sara's room in the wee hours.

As she hung the last clean curtain at the drawing room window Sara heard Maura's voice behind her.

"I need to talk to you mother," she said in a strained voice. Getting down from the chair Sara looked at her daughter, the expression on her face brought a sense of foreboding to the pit of her stomach.

"What is it Maura?" she asked. "I have decided to go back to Clougher and take Mary Kate with me. I've tried to fit in here. But it just isn't home for me." Tears filled her eyes, as she looked away from her mother's pained gaze.

"We want you to come with us. I want us to be like a family again."

"You know that I just can't get up and leave Jean like that. And you also know well how parting with Mary Kate will break my heart."

As Maura looked away from her mother's eyes, Sara

sensed oceans of uncertainty between them.

"I'm sorry mother, but I don't feel at home here, and Mary Kate is all I have left."

"She is not a possession you know," she said angrily. For the first time in her life Maura saw resentment in her mother's face. "I ask only one thing from you Maura," she went on. "If you must do this, I ask only one thing."

They looked at each other in silence for a while, then Maura asked, "what is the one thing?"

"That you will always put Mary Kate's happiness first." Maura nodded.

"I'm sorry for all the heartache I have caused you," she said, looking at her mother's tear stained face with pleading eyes.

Sara walked over to where she stood and held out her arms, as they hugged each other Sara said quietly, "I will help you to pack her things. But you can't take a child into that damp house Maura."

"I wrote to Grace Murphy a few weeks ago, and I had a reply from her yesterday. She will have the house aired for us."

"Grace is a good woman. At least you will have one friend in Clougher."

Sara sat alone at the window in the nursery on her return from the station. Jean stayed downstairs knowing that she was in no mood for company. She felt the dusk growing in the room about her, until the cot and rocking horse became mere shadows. Suddenly from her throat an anguished wail filled the dusky gloom.

"Mary Kate, Mary Kate," she repeated.

She suddenly wished that she had James to talk to, drunk or sober, but even he had deserted. Somehow the night wore in, and as she watched the dawn break she knew that her sense of loss had not abated. Jean was already in the kitchen when Sara opened the door.

"Good morning Sara. How are you?"

"I'm all right," she replied with a smile. But the smile failed to hide the sadness from Jean. Jean put the pot of tea on the table and poured two cups. They sipped the tea in silence for a while, then Jean said.

"Sara, I want you to go home to Clougher. Your place is with your daughter and the wee one. I'm no fool. You are staying here because you don't want to leave me. And any fool can see that it's breaking your heart."

"You're only right on one count Jean. True, I wouldn't want to leave you on your own. But..." Before she had a chance to finish Jean broke in.

"I know a very good home for people in my position where I would be well looked after. It's in Dublin, and I would be perfectly happy to live out my days there. So you see Sara..."

"Will you give over Jean and let me finish what I was saying," Sara said, putting up her hand to stop Jean from interrupting. "In the first place I don't want to go back to Clougher. And in the second place Maura doesn't want me there. Oh, I know she asked me to go with her. But she wants to bring up Mary Kate on her own." She sipped the tea and stared into space for a while before going on, "do you know Jean that for the first time in my life I don't care a hoot about what becomes of Maura. It's Mary Kate's happiness that I care about most now, and I know that the wee soul will miss us. That's what grieves me."

Jean watched in sadness as the tears slid down Sara's cheeks and she felt her own eyes fill as the knowledge sunk in, that maybe never again would she see Mary Kate's happy little face, and that a light had been cruelly snuffed out of their lives. Reaching across she touched Sara's hand desperately struggling to bring her a morsel of comfort. Then she said, "James might bring us good news."

It was late evening when Maura and Mary Kate arrived in Clougher. The house had been newly whitewashed and a thin smoke wafted from the chimney. Almost as soon as the taxi drew up the door opened and Grace Murphy greeted them with a smile and a hug.

"Welcome home. And you must be Mary Kate," she said warmly bending down to give her a hug.
Mary Kate's eyes stared back sullenly as she backed away from her embrace. Maura surveyed the kitchen with pleasure, she could scarcely believe the change for the better since her last visit.

"You must have worked so hard Grace. How can I ever thank you."

"Think nothing of it, it was my pleasure."

Then from behind the chair by the fire they heard whimpering sounds. Mary Kate sat in a little heap on the floor, her small body heaving with low sounding sobs.

"What's wrong pet?" Maura asked, gathering her up in her arms.

"Want home to Nana."

"But this is your new home. Remember I told you all about it."

"Don't like it. I want to go home," she sobbed.

"Poor wee soul this is all strange to her," Grace said sympathetically. Then she said, "Sara will be missing her just as much, if I know Sara. The last few times I saw her she talked non stop about Mary Kate."

Maura could feel resentment rising up as she listened, and she had to struggle to keep it under control.

"She will be fine in the morning," Maura answered a little sharply, then almost immediately regretted her tone.

When Grace bid her goodnight and they were alone Maura felt a sudden panic. The silence of the house seemed to mock her. The only sound came from the occasional quiet sobs of the dozing child. Maura's thoughts went back to the last night she had spent under this roof. She remembered lying rigid and sleepless in bed, terrified about the frightening unknown that lay ahead. But as always her thoughts went back to Andrew. And she was seized, by a deep longing to see him just once more. And as she faced up to the fact that she would never see him again, the pain was almost unbearable. The memories of her time in New York seemed so distant now as she sat in the twilight, watching the turf fire slowly die. She read again Hannah's letters in her mind, and envied her busy successful life. 'But I still have you Mary Kate,' she whispered softly as she gazed fondly at her sleeping child.

Chapter 14

The Meeting

James Thompson sat alone on the deck of the ship deep in his own thoughts. Tomorrow they would dock in New York, and he suddenly felt apprehensive about what he had travelled all this way to do. The full moon trailing long black shadows on the water brought thoughts of his honeymoon back to haunt him. He remembered how happy they had been then, when he had last sailed to New York. They had been two young people in love, with their future stretching out endlessly in front of them. As tears filled his eyes and dropped down his face, it dawned on him that this was the first time that he had cried since she died on that long ago winter's night. Instead of tears, he had grieved in a towering drunken rage. He could smell her scent and feel the nearness of her, in a way he couldn't understand. He sat motionless while tears continued to rain down his face, and in some strange way this state felt comforting. He felt suddenly at peace with himself, and that he had at last come to terms with her loss.

The pink flush of dawn stole over the ocean before

he left the deck and went down to his cabin. He slept without the aid of whiskey for the first time in years.

James made his way down Thirty-first Street carrying his suitcase through the crowded street. Children played on the sidewalks, piercing the iron sound of traffic with laughter, and here and there old men sat on the fire escapes soaking up the morning sun. He stopped halfway down the block and looked up at a tall drab building with a boarding house sign above the door. Once inside he lifted the dirty brass bell from the counter and shook it. He listened as it's echoes trembled away into silence. A large drably dressed woman appeared in the doorway. "Yeah?"

"Have you any rooms to let?"

"Yeah, there's a couple left," she answered, walking over to the board on the wall with two keys hanging from it.

"How much?" he asked.

"Three bucks a night. If you want the tub, it's a buck extra."

He followed her up the creaky dark stairway with it's pealing paintwork until they reached a door on the landing. Inside the room looked much as he imagined it would. The walls were grimy and a limp lace curtain hung at the small window overlooking the grim street below.

"I'll take it for three nights," he said.

"That's nine bucks without the tub," she replied holding out her hand." He handed her ten dollars.

"I'll be needing the tub."

When she had gone he glanced at his watch; it said eleven thirty. 'Might as well go today and get it over with,' he muttered to himself, throwing the suitcase on the bed. Back out on the street, bathed and changed, he felt some of the gloom from the grimy boarding house leave him. He wished that he could have afforded somewhere a little better, but he reminded himself that his three day stay would soon pass, and he was pleased that he had managed to book the return passage in such a short time.

With a little help from passers by, he soon found himself looking up at the 'Jefferson Shipping Company' offices in the smart commercial area of Manhattan. He brushed himself down and walked up the stairs at a smart pace while his courage remained. From behind a desk in the spacious outer office, a young receptionist looked up as he entered.

"Can I help you?"

"I have come to see Andrew Jefferson."

"Have you an appointment sir?"

"No. But I think he will see me anyway."

"Mister Jefferson sees no one without an appointment."

"That may normally be so. But I think he will see me," he said, before she had time to protest. "Tell him that James Thompson is here to talk to him about Maura Quinn, please," he added with a smile.

"Sit down over there, and I'll ask if he will see you," she said pointing to a group of chairs against the far wall.

As he sat alone he felt nervous and anxious. If he did agree to see him, where would he begin? Just then the receptionist returned.

"Mr. Jefferson will see you shortly Mr. Thompson," she said with a note of surprise in her voice. A few minutes later, he was shown into Andrew Jefferson's, spacious, and beautifully furnished office by his secretary. For an instant neither man moved or spoke, standing perfectly still they stared at each other. James swallowed hard and cleared his throat before he spoke.

"I'm James Thompson from Donegal in Ireland," he said with a smile as he held out his hand.

Andrew shook his hand firmly, "I'm pleased to meet you Mr Thompson. Please sit down."

"James, call me James."

"I have been told that your visit is something to do with Maura Quinn. How can I help you?" As they sat facing each other James felt a shiver of fear sweep over him; the man seemed coldly indifferent. What if she got this all wrong, and the true love thing was all one sided, he had to find out, and quick.

"Can I ask you a personal question Mr. Jefferson?"

"Andrew," he interrupted with a nod. "What is your....er feelings for Maura Quinn?" James watched his face closely during the silent pause that followed. His countenance took on a look of anxiety before he asked.

"Is she all right?"

"Physically, yes. But emotionally no, and that is why I'm here."

Andrew looked away from James for a while.

"You wanted to know what my feelings were for her," he said, looking back at James.

"She was a young girl I befriended, and fell in love with... foolishly with hindsight. Did you come all this way to ask me that?"

"No... I came because I owe Maura's mother a great debt. And also because I couldn't bear to see a young girl so unhappy."

"I am not the reason for her unhappiness. I wanted to marry her. But she in effect turned me down. I didn't get an answer to any of my letters...so naturally I gave up on her and got on with my life," he said, with a shrug of his shoulders.

"The reasons for this will become clear, if you will allow me to tell her story."

"Did she send you here?"

"No. She doesn't know I'm here...I took this upon myself."

Getting up from the chair he went to the door and called his secretary. A couple of minutes later he came back and sat down again.

"I have ordered coffee," he announced. James found himself relaxing a little as he warmed to this big man seated opposite. "How long do you plan to stay in New York?" James he asked

"Oh, just three days. I managed to book a passage back on the Empress on Thursday."

"You won't have much time to explore the sights in such a short while."

A knock at the door interrupted them. Getting up again he opened the door to his secretary carrying a tray of coffee and sandwiches. "I don't want any interruptions for the next hour or so," he said, as she got to the door.

When they had eaten the sandwiches and drank the coffee, Andrew offered him a cigarette.

"Thanks. Well I suppose I had better begin the story that I crossed the Atlantic to tell you."

Andrew gave him a smile of encouragement, and he began a little nervously at first. As he talked Andrew remained silent.

When James finished his story, there was silence in the room. He could hear the faint noises from the streets below, and tried to concentrate on identifying the sounds to take his mind from the tension in the room.

Getting up from the chair silently, Andrew walked up and down the floor, just as he always did when faced with the unexpected. Seated silently in the big leather chair James felt anxiety and fear creep over him. Finally he came back and sat down opposite him again. With a shaking hand he handed him the photograph of Mary Kate that he always carried with him. Andrew gazed at it in silence for what seemed like an eternity, while James recited bits of half forgotten prayers. At last he spoke.

"So this is Mary Kate. She is beautiful like her mother," he said quietly, raising his gaze from the photograph to meet the anxious eyes of James Thompson, then he said.

"Poor little Maura. For once I am lost for words."

"I'm sorry Mr. Jefferson, maybe I shouldn't have told you."

"Andrew, I told you to call me Andrew," he said before he went on.

"I always knew there was something. But in my wildest dreams I didn't expect anything as mammoth as this. But as far as telling me is concerned, I'm glad you did," he spoke with gentleness. "What happened to her was tragic, cruel, sad. But it doesn't make a whit of difference to the way I feel about her. I am only sorry that she had so little faith in me," he added with a sigh.

James felt as if a tightly held valve had been released in his head, and relief flooded through him.

Then looking at James he said, "I'm not quite sure what I should do now. I need time to think."

"I understand. I'll leave you now," James said getting up from the chair.

"Not so fast. Where are you staying?"

"Oh....just a small hotel, it's only for three nights. Just took the first place I came to."

"We can't have that. I will send my motorcar to collect your luggage."

"No. I'll be fine."

"I won't take no for an answer, and my mother will be glad of the company."

"Well in that case thank you very much. Could I meet you back here in say two hours? I have a call to make and I will collect the luggage on the way back."

"Ok.. I will see you in two hours."

James breathed a sigh of relief as he walked back down to the street. He didn't want him to see the dingy boarding house. His feet felt light as he retraced his steps, well satisfied with his morning's work. In fact he felt lighter and happier than he had done in years . As he walked back towards the boarding house he noticed the same children playing in the street, only this time it all looked less, drab in his eyes. A small girl walked close to him with brown curly hair, she reminded him of Mary Kate. On impulse he reached out and put his hand on her soft curls, and was consumed with a deep longing to see Mary Kate again.

When James left the office Andrew sat motionless in his chair pondering on the unexpected news that this stranger had brought. He had thought that he had put Maura Quinn firmly into the past; but now he wasn't so sure. His head was full of thoughts of her, the sadness in her eyes as she boarded the ship that day came back to haunt him. Suddenly he knew that he had to see her again.

Chapter 15

Facing the Past

Maura sat by the hearth close to the fire and listened to the wind rattle the windows. Above the noise of the wind she heard a loud knock. With her heart thumping in her ears she stood behind the door.

"Who's there?" she called.

"It's me, Ellen Murphy," the voice came back above the noise of the wind. Maura opened the door with a sigh of relief.

"I'm so glad to see you," she said with a smile of welcome.

"You must have guessed that I'm in need of company."

Seated across the hearth from Ellen, Maura felt close to tears. The three weeks since her return to Clougher had seemed like forever; so great was her loneliness and sense of isolation. And to add to her gloom, the rain had not ceased in days. Mary Kate had lost her sparkle, her face had become waxen and she hardly ever laughed anymore. Maura had become more and more anxious about her with each passing day, and had to accept that she was not going to settle in Clougher.

"Well, how are you getting on?" Ellen asked.

"I'm not. That is everything has gone wrong, nothing has turned out the way I planned." Ellen listened attentively as Maura told her about her miserable time since she returned home. "What am I going to do Ellen?" she asked, with a note of desperation." Living here has only made me feel worse... Every time I look out the window I am reminded of him. He ruined my life." Ellen looked into the fire for a few seconds before she spoke.

"I was his victim too. I had to put his awful memory as far away into the background as possible. You must do the same Maura."

"That's easier said than done." Maura said quietly.

"His evil can only win victory over you if you let it.Did I tell you Maura that I am engaged to Michael Connell?" Maura shook her head. "I told him about what happened to me. I didn't want there to be any secrets between us."

"What did he say?"

"Oh, he wanted to try to find him so as he could kill him." Ellen said. "But when he calmed down we just cried together. He reassured me that it made no difference to the way he felt about me. No. No, difference at all. Listen to me Maura, you must stop feeling sorry for yourself and get on with your life."

Ellen's gentle face and pale quiet eyes lulled Maura into a state of tranquillity, that lasted long after she had gone, and slumber fell on her tired eyelids as she was lulled to sleep to the sound of the rain on the windows.

Mary Kate's cries woke her up, and she was again confronted with her mounting problem of her child's unhappiness and nightly fits of crying. As she cuddled her and soothed her fears her mother's words came back to her. 'Always put Mary Kate's happiness first.'

"It's all right love. I'm taking you home to Nana tomorrow."

The morning sun shone brightly as Maura stood waiting for the trap to collect them for the station. Mary Kate danced and skipped on the doorstep so great was her delight at going home. As Maura watched she knew that she was doing the right thing. Standing there Maura's thoughts went back over the past; to her childhood, to her father, and she again shuddered as she looked up the lane to Seamus' derelict house. Then her thoughts went back to Andrew, his face came into her memory as though he were standing next to her, and again she felt the sharp tug of longing. The present, on the contrary, seemed to grow a little hazy, to slip away, and not one thing concerning the future brought her any comfort. She knew that even though she may never see Andrew again she also knew that the strands of her life were interwoven with his; and that even time and the world could not part them altogether. With this thought she helped Mary Kate into the trap that would take them to the station, and take her beloved Mary

Kate home.

As she filled the basket of turf for the evening Sara heard the sound of a trap in the front drive. Her heart leapt with joy when she saw them. Then Mary Kate ran with her small arms outstretched. "Nana, Nana," she called excitedly.

"My wee precious; you're home," Sara's voice choked with emotion as she held her small body close to her own. Then looking at Maura she said, "I'm so glad...so very glad that you have both come home."

"I'm not sure where I belong or where I go from here. But I know now that Mary Kate belongs here."

"There is a place for you here too Maura," Sara said, putting her free arm around her shoulder.

In the drawing room Jean sat dozing by the fire. Sara shook her gently by the shoulder. "Look who's here." Rubbing her eyes she looked up at Sara. When she saw Mary Kate in her arms her kindly craggy old face lit up with joy.

"Mary Kate, Mary Kate, darling you're home." Wiggling out of Sara's arms she ran to Jean, and then climbing on to her knee she put her small arms around her neck, she kissed her wrinkled old face now wet with tears. As Maura watched she could feel goose--pimples rising on her neck, and felt happy in the knowledge that she had made the three people most dear to her heart happy.

Maura gathered the last few potatoes that she had dug and

threw them into the bucket. Straightening up she looked beyond the stone wall to where her mother was hanging sheets on the line. She continued to watch as Mary Kate handed her the clothes pegs as she needed them, then she saw her mother pick the child up in her arms, then swinging her around she laughed as she kissed her on both cheeks. As she picked up the bucket and headed for the kitchen, she tried to control the pangs of jealousy that swept over her.

She found Jean sitting at the kitchen table drinking a cup of tea.

"The tea's still hot if you want a cup," Jean said, as she came in. Did you happen to see the postman anywhere?" Jean asked her.

"No, not a sign of him."

"Are you expecting a letter?"

"Not really. I just always hope for mail. Are you feeling any more settled dear?" Maura shook her head.

"I have been thinking about going back to America. I thought about trying Boston this time...I have to try to make a life of my own."
Jean looked at her in silence for a while. Then she said, "Maura wait a few weeks before you come to any definite decisions. Will you promise me that, after all what's a few weeks when all is said and done?"

"I had planned to go to Derry on Monday to book the passage. I think I have hung around long enough." Reaching across the table Jean took Maura's hand in hers, then she said,

"Just a few weeks more, eh? Trust me."

"I'll think about it," Maura replied, but she couldn't help feeling that Jean was being a bit mysterious.

In the days ahead Maura felt that small dreams beckoned her, but she made no move to transform them into realities. Why, she could not have told. She felt as if she were floating upon a sea strange and uncertain which tossed her hither and thither and bore her to no definite haven. A week later in a more positive frame of mind, Maura came to a decision about her future. She would go to Derry and book her passage without telling either her mother or Jean.

"It will be easier for all concerned if I tell them the night before my departure," she told herself.

A good opportunity to kill two birds with one stone came the following evening when they were discussing what to do about the house and farm in Clougher.

"We could rent it out easy enough I suppose," Sara suggested. "Do you remember me telling you that Ellen Murphy is getting married and looking for a place to live? Well, how about renting the house out to them?"

"That's a great idea Maura. And I know your father would approve. She was very good to him," she smiled at Maura and sighed softly. "It might be a good idea to offer the land for rent to her father while you are about it. If he wants it that would solve two problems in one."

"I'll go tomorrow morning and see," Maura

answered, but all the while she was planning her trip to Derry. Half an hour should conclude the business in Clougher, then she could go on to Derry. As she looked at her mother's smiling face a sudden rush of guilt swept over her.

Mary Kate slept peacefully on her mother's lap, her brown curls framing her pretty face. The sadness she felt at parting from her stabbed at her heart like a knife. But she knew there was no turning back.

Chapter 16

Crossing the Atlantic

Two hours later James Thompson found himself back at the Jefferson Shipping Company offices. He met Andrew in the lobby, as he was about to make his way back up to his office.

"Glad I caught you. The car is waiting out front," Andrew said cheerfully.

"I hope your mother won't mind having an unexpected guest thrust upon her," James commented as they got into the car.

"Not at all, she's delighted. I told her already," he reassured him with a lopsided grin. "I usually stay in town during weekdays, and I think my mother gets a little lonely. So you see she was delighted when I told her not only to expect me, but also a guest."

As the car swept through the driveway James felt a little apprehensive, and for the first time since he left Derry he felt a strong need for a stiff whiskey.

Andrew's mother was a warm friendly woman, and he

soon felt at home in her company. The evening was filled with chatter light as the iridescent bubbles that float from a bubble pipe. But when Andrew went to answer the telephone and they were alone together she asked.

"How is Maura? What possessed her to run off like that?" Before he had time to answer she went on. "Andrew was very cut up about it you know. Oh, he never said much to me, but I knew." Then looking away from him she said. "I was very fond of her."

"I have explained the reasons for her leaving to Andrew." But before he could say anymore Andrew reappeared.

"Can you postpone your return to Ireland by three days James?" he asked from the doorway.

"I'm sorry but I don't think I can. You see, as I explained I have booked the return passage for Friday."

"Let me explain. I have decided to go to Ireland with you. But I can't get away until next Tuesday. I would like us to travel together and if you agree I can book us both on the Louise. One of the perks of being in the shipping business." he added with a grin.

"Well.... in that case I can wait for the few extra days." James said trying to hide his relief. Then right on the heels of elation came panic. What would he do for money? As he listened to Mrs. Jefferson make plans about how she would show him the sights of New York, James felt the sudden nervous stroke of his heart as he thought about the last twenty dollars in his wallet. His hand brushing past the chain of his pocket watch gave him the answer to his dilemma, 'I will pawn it in the morning,' he thought suddenly with relief. The watch was the last thing of value he possessed; a gift from his father, on his twenty first birthday. But it was in a good cause, probably the best cause that would ever come his way. So with a renewed sense of relief he found himself relaxing, and he began to look forward to the extra unexpected time in New York.

During the days that followed he got to know Andrew Jefferson's mother very well. She talked about her late husband and family at length. The special light that came into her eyes when she mentioned Andrew made it plain to James that he was her favourite son. "I'm going to miss you tomorrow James," she said while she poured him a glass of sherry.

"And I will miss you. I've enjoyed these few days more than I can say," he said.

"Promise me that you will come back soon," she said leaning towards him. He smiled at her, then taking her hand in his he said, "I'll do my best." As he looked around the house with all it's luxury and affluence he couldn't help wondering how she felt about the possible prospect of having a penniless Irish girl for a daughter-in-law.

"You were very brave to come all this way, and I know Andrew is very grateful to you."

"And what about you Mrs. Jefferson?"

"I am also grateful to you. I hope that whatever came between them can be mended." Then gazing out the window her next words made him think, that she had read his thoughts.

"If I had been asked ten years ago what the ideal wife for Andrew would be, I would probably have said someone from the same social background." Then looking him straight in the eye she went on. "I have learned a lot about people and what is really important in these last two years. You know, when I watched Maura with my young grandson and saw the love and affection she showed him when his own mother ignored him, I learned about what is really important in life. Poor Maura had a raw deal with the Jeffersons. Locked away in that house with an evil mad woman... and still she showed love and affection to all of us. I hope it works out for both of them, I really do," she added with a gentle smile.

"That's very comforting to know," James said, suddenly feeling that the day was worthwhile a singing day dusted with gold.

As James settled into his first class cabin for the homeward journey, he couldn't help comparing the striking contrast with his outward journey in the cramped second class conditions. From the bottom of his suitcase he took out Mary Kate's photograph, then sitting down on the chair he gazed at it and was seized by a deep longing to see her again.

"What ever comes out of this, I hope that we won't loose you," he whispered to the empty cabin. Glancing at the open suitcase he saw the whiskey bottle. Getting up from the chair he went over and lifted it out, holding it at eye level, he gazed at the amber liquid before removing the cork, then almost immediately he replaced it again before tossing the bottle back into the suitcase and closing it with his foot. He swiftly left the cabin and went out on deck relieved that he had resisted the strong temptation of the whiskey. He knew only too well that once he started the whiskey he wouldn't be able to stop. Once out on deck he gulped the sea air, slowly filling his lungs until he felt his body relax. Ahead of the ship a red sunset had spread across the sky, to the east grey honey-coloured clouds were massing bringing the night with them.

"Oh, there you are. I am just about to go to the dining room." Andrew's voice coming from behind startled him.

"Fine, I'll join you." James said, following him down the steps. Over the meal James said. "I'm a bit edgy now that we are on our way. What if it doesn't work out and I've taken you on a wild goose chase?"

"Don't worry about that. If it doesn't work out it won't be your fault. I've got to find out one way or the other. If you hadn't come on the scene I could well have spent the rest of my life wondering. Now relax and enjoy the voyage."

Looking around him James thought that as he was never likely to travel in this luxury again, he might as well enjoy it.

A few days into the journey he was becoming anxious again. 'Would Maura be there? Would they all be well at home? Around and around his thoughts went when he was trying to sleep, and he was tempted over and over again to seek refuge in the whiskey bottle. He wrote out the telegram message he would send to Aunt Jean when they reached Liverpool.

On the fourth evening of the voyage a storm blew up suddenly out of a clear blue evening sky. That evening, the dining room was almost deserted; most of the passengers having gone down to their cabins. James followed Andrew somewhat unsteadily to their respective cabins, while the ship lurched and tossed beneath them. James fell into an uneasy sleep in the wee hours. He awoke from a bad dream shaking and perspiring. The dream had been so real to him that he had to pinch himself to prove that it had just been a dream. He had dreamt that Maura and Andrew were taking Mary Kate away from them. They were standing on the quayside and Mary Kate was in Sara's arms when she was wrenched away from her. The sound of the child screaming in protest still rang loud in his ears as he sat on the edge of his bunk while the ship still lurched and tossed in the gale. Going over to the suitcase he opened it and rummaged around until he found the whiskey bottle, he was about to close it when he saw the child's photograph staring back at him from the jumble of clothing. Again he tossed the bottle back into the case.
Out on deck the rising sun coloured the clouds with pale

shades of crimson. As he watched his spirits lifted and the nightmare faded.

Chapter 17

The Telegram

Jean stuffed the telegram hurriedly into her apron pocket when Sara came into the kitchen. Sara knew, by the way she averted her eyes that she was hiding something.

"Did you get a letter?" Sara asked.
Jean went back to peeling the potatoes before she answered.

"No, I was just reading an old letter," she said, not taking her eyes from her work.

"Come on, I know when you are lying. Is it news about James? You might as well tell me," she said defiantly, sitting down opposite her. Jean looked up at her, and the defiant look in her eyes told her there was no escape. She would have to tell her.

"Where is Maura?" she asked in a hushed voice.

"Down at the shore with Mary Kate." She sighed deeply before she spoke again. "I don't know where to begin Sara. But...before I tell you anything, you must promise me that not a word of what I am going to tell you will be uttered to Maura." Her expression told Sara that without the promise she would get nothing out of her.

"All right, I promise."

"James went to New York to see Andrew Jefferson. Now before you say anything, it was as much my idea as his. You see.... we couldn't, bear to see the poor girl so miserable." She looked at Sara's startled shocked expression, and felt deflated. Then licking her dry lips she went on. "The telegram was from James. They have arrived in Liverpool. Andrew Jefferson is with him. They will be here in three days." She watched Sara get up from the table and walk to the window in silence. When she could stand the silence no longer she said, "For God's sake, say something Sara."

Turning from the window Sara came back and sat down again facing Jean. As their gazes met Jean could hear her own heart pounding in her breast. Then at last Sara said, "if they are to arrive in three days we had better get to work. The bedrooms will need cleaning and airing."

"Oh, Sara you nearly gave me heart failure. I thought that you were angry, that we had done the wrong thing."

"Well, that will teach you not to keep secrets from me again. I knew all along that you were keeping something from me. But I must confess that I never guessed...that it was anything like this," she said, with a shake of her head.

Maura watched while Mary Kate gathered tiny pink shells

on the beach. She was all too conscious of how little time she had left to spend with her. "The day after tomorrow I'll be on my way, to God knows where," she said aloud with a shudder.

"What did you say Mammy?" Mary Kate asked as she came towards her. Maura gathered her into her arms and sunk her head in her curls. "Remember I will always love you no matter what," she said gently. Then getting up she took her by the hand, and they made their way slowly up the path.

The following afternoon Jean watched Sara leave in the trap for the village shops as usual. When she had gone she went up to her room for her afternoon nap. She was awakened a short time later by the sound of a motor engine. As her mind became more alert a sudden thought struck her. 'Could they have come a day early?' she wondered. Getting out of bed, she went over to the window. She could see nothing. Going to the door she opened it and went out to the landing. Then she heard Maura's voice coming from the direction of the stairs. She slid back into her room quietly and listened as the voices came closer along the landing. Then she heard Maura say in a hushed voice.

"Remember, pick me up at the gates tomorrow at two. Don't come to the house. Take the trunk now, and leave it with the station master." She remained behind the door until she heard them going back down the stairs.

Then she went quickly to the back bedroom overlooking the back yard. She watched them load the trunk into Johnny Molloy's hackney car with disbelief. It was now obvious to her that Maura intended leaving the following afternoon. She slowly and stiffly lowered herself unto her knees. 'Dear Lord, please don't let this happen. Help me to find a way to keep her here for just a few days longer,' she repeated over and over.

Back in her own room she lay motionless on the bed while her thoughts ran amock in her head. She had thought about little else in weeks, and now when success seemed just around the corner it was all going wrong. If only she had succeeded in making these two young people happy, then she would have felt that she had done something really worthwhile in her declining years. Somehow Jean felt that she was reliving her own youth through Maura; regaining her own lost love. She suddenly felt deflated, old and tired, she closed her eyes and tried to shut out the bitter disappointment that seemed to have totally drained her.

It was the sound of the wind that woke Jean from her sleep. It had a deep hollow whine that seemed to come from the bowels of the sea in a ghostly echoing note as it howled and rattled around the old house. She lay listening to the storm for a while before she remembered about Maura and the trunk. Then she saw the flicker of a light under the door.

"Are you all right Jean?" Sara called out from the open doorway.

"I'm all right."

She put the candle on the bedside table and busied herself pulling the curtains across the window. "God above what a night. I hope to the good Lord that James and Andrew are not on the Irish sea on a night like this," she said, as she pulled the quilt around Jeans shoulders.

"I hope not too. But they will be too late anyway," she added with a sigh. "She's for off in the morning. I found out this afternoon when I saw the trunk being loaded into the hackney car." Grabbing Sara by the arm she said with a sob in her voice. "I wanted to do this one thing right before I died. Wouldn't you think that I would have been granted that one last wish?"

"She told me tonight at bedtime that she was going to Boston tomorrow." Sara said, as she stroked Jean's forehead. "But all is not lost yet. It's a wild night out there, and my guess is that no ships will go anywhere for a day or two."

"Sara I find you a constant wonder. You have a way of making the worst scenario seem... somehow to be all right." In the flickering candle- light Sara could see hope in her tired old eyes.

"Like a mug of hot milk?" she asked.

"Only if you're making one for yourself."

"Aye, I'm making one for myself."

Later as she sipped the comforting hot milk, Jean thought

that the storm didn't sound as fearful nor the future so bleak as it had done half an hour ago.

At daybreak the storm still raged as Sara surveyed the house for damage. Holding on to the wall she managed to anchor herself long enough to get a view of the roof to satisfy herself that it was still intact. In some strange way she felt a kinship with the old house. She felt that if the house could weather storms then she could weather them also; it represented security to her, and as to why she felt this way about a house that didn't even belong to her, she could not attempt to explain.

By mid-day the storm had died down a little; the gusts of wind were a little less fierce. At one o'clock Maura came into the kitchen with her coat under her arm.

"Where you going Mammy?" Mary Kate asked, lifting her up into her arms, she said,

"Mammy's going away for a while precious. But I'll write to you every day, and I'll be back soon."

"I don't want you to go," she said sullenly.
Sara listened with a sinking feeling that reached the very pit of her stomach. She knew that she had to think of something fast. Then she said, "you won't get far today Maura. Henry says that the railway lines are blocked by fallen trees," she lied. "And anyway there will be no sailing's for a day or two." Maura walked over to the window and stared out silently, then with a deep sigh she turned to face Sara. "I wanted to get this over with now,

the...parting." She sat down at the head of the table dejectedly with her head in her hands, then she said, "I didn't sleep last night dreading the parting. And now I will have to go through this again tomorrow."

"Maybe it's providence love," Sara said, with a sigh of relief.

"I wouldn't call it that, more like somebody up there having it in for me," she said dejectedly. Then taking Mary Kate by the hand she left the kitchen.

When she had gone Sara slumped down in the nearest chair making a noise of exasperation. She knew that she had bought one more day by lying to her, but she wondered now if it had been worth it. She knew that if they hadn't turned up by tomorrow she would be forced to tell her about Andrew's arrival.

When Sara got up the following morning she noticed Maura's door was ajar. She poked her head around the door and saw that it was neat and tidy, and empty. She was about to leave when she caught sight of the white envelope on the pillow. Before she opened it she knew with a sinking heart that she was gone. She sat on the bed for ages before she opened the letter, and when she read it her whole body shook with sobs. Finally she dried her eyes on her apron and went across the landing to break the news to Jean.

Chapter 18

To Love Again

Leaving James to rest in the hotel, Andrew Jefferson wandered along Derry quayside killing time until the train was due. His attention was drawn to a young woman sitting alone on a bench; something about her looked familiar, drawing him closer to where she sat. Staring down at her unobserved he felt his heart quicken as he was seized by a sudden rush of love for her, and he knew at that moment how right he had been to make this journey. She suddenly looked up, startled recognition blazing in her amber eyes. "Andrew...what.........how ....did you get here?"

"To find you of course," he said smiling tenderly down at her. "And I'm not leaving without you." Then reaching down he gathered her small hands in his big ones and pulled her gently to her feet. Folding his arms around her he kissed her for all that had been between them and for everything that was yet to come.

Maura's face became suffused with happiness as she gazed

up at him. Then she said quietly, "Andrew, you don't know about the past."

"The past is gone Maura. Only the future counts. But tell me what you are doing here?"

"I set out this morning with the intention of sailing across the Atlantic. I was going to Boston," she said in a shaking voice.

"Merciful God. Fate has been kind to us then. I only found you by accident," he said quietly, leading her back to the bench.

They sat on the bench with their arms around each other, each savouring the joy of the other's nearness, until Andrew remembered that it was almost time for the train.

Back at the hotel James Thompson looked anxiously at the clock above the desk. His heart leapt with joy when he saw them coming through the door hand in hand, with broad smiles beaming on their happy faces. Maura ran up to him, tears, springing into her eyes as she threw her arms around him. "Thank you, thank you," she repeated. He patted her on the shoulder, while he smiled back at Andrew.

Jean had spent most of the day in bed staring gloomily into space. Sara brought Mary Kate up to her room in the afternoon, hoping to stir her out of her gloom. "Listen Jean, you are going to have to look after the wee one for me for a while. She's missing... you know who," she finished in a near whisper. Jean looked down at Mary

Kate and smiled tenderly. Then reaching out her arms, she said. "Come on darling; come and snuggle down beside me. Now, what would you like to do? Would you like me to read to you?" When she had scurried off to find her books, she looked at Sara and said quietly. "Do you know Sara; I love her more than I have ever loved anyone, or anything in my life." Taking the lace hankie from the bedside table, Sara wiped the tears from her eyes. "I know, I know Jean."

With a smile of satisfaction she watched them from the doorway; their heads close together, totally absorbed in the books that James had made for her. As she watched she was amazed all over again at the closeness between them, a friendship between the very young and the very old. Then she closed the door quietly and went about her work.

Sara heard the noise of a motor car engine, and went over to the sitting room window to investigate. She saw James first as he got out of the car, followed by Maura and a tall handsome looking man whom she guessed was Andrew Jefferson. Her joy at seeing James again took her by surprise; she had missed him more than she had dared to admit. He stood in the doorway as soon as she opened it.

"Welcome home." she said quietly.

"I've missed you. I'm glad to be home," he said with a gentle smile.

Then from behind her Mary Kate called out as she ran past

Sara. "Uncle James, Uncle James," she repeated, bumping into Sara in her excitement.
Lifting her up in his arms he buried his head in her hair.

"I can't tell you how much I've missed you."
Then turning to Sara, he said with emotion in his voice.

"I have to confess to missing this little angel most of all." Then moving her head back into a position where she could look into his eyes Mary Kate asked. "Will you make me more books?"

"Nothing like getting your orders in quick, eh, Mary Kate," he said with a broad smile of pleasure.
Turning her attention to Andrew she held out her hand in greeting.

"Welcome," she said with a smile.
He smiled down at her, his blue eyes crinkling at the corners.

"I can't tell you how glad I am to be here," he said. She liked this big man instantly; she liked his kindly honest eyes, and firm handshake, and had a sixth sense that told her Maura's future was in good hands.

During the following days Sara, Andrew and Jean watched with feelings of joy as the young couple wandered around the place totally wrapped up in one another. Their love for each other became apparent to them all as the days passed. They each in turn tried to cope with the almost unbearable thought of losing Mary Kate, it was as if each moment spent with her became very precious, while at the same time trying to protect their emotions with an armour against the pain of losing her.

Over dinner James took delight in the new atmosphere of the house, the dining room was being used again, the old furniture shone with beeswax, and the silver glistened in the candle-light.

Presiding at the head of the table he watched approvingly at the loving glances that passed between Andrew and Maura. Then looking across at Sara, he studied her face as if she were a very interesting person he had just met. She had weathered well in spite of everything. Her skin glowed, and time had softened the lines on her face. He'd been lucky not to lose this woman. Luckier than he deserved.

When she had cleared the table Sara was overcome with the need to go upstairs to see Mary Kate. Sitting in the nursery she caressed her hair gently. Then she heard the door open behind her. Before she could see him, she knew that it was James. Coming over to the bedside he whispered, "has she said anything yet?" Shaking her head, she looked at his concerned face now beginning to blur and waver through her tears. "What will we do if they take her away from us?"

Patting his hand on her shoulder he answered in a quivering voice, "I don't know Sara. I don't know." Then touching Mary Kate's head gently he left the room.

This was a time of miracles for Maura. She blossomed as her love for Andrew grew with each passing day. They walked through the glens and along the shores hand in hand, with only thoughts for each other.

With arms linked they walked up the path from the shore, as they neared the top of the cliff Andrew suddenly said, "You haven't told me about what you want to happen to Mary Kate yet." Maura stopped on the path a look of concern crossing her face.

"Andrew that is the only fear I have had since you came." Putting a comforting arm around her shoulder he said gently, I can't advise you on what to do on this one. The decision has to be yours alone." Looking away from her he stared down the valley, and straight ahead at the broad sweep of the Atlantic. He watched the smoke gently rising from the chimneys of the snug white cottages tucked under the hillsides. "This is a magic land Maura. No matter what you decide about Mary Kate's future, I'm determined to return here again and again; every summer in fact." Then turning to Maura he kissed her hard on the lips.

"Andrew do you really mean that."

"Are you asking about the kiss, or about our coming back every summer?"

"About our coming back every year."

"Of course I mean it." Then looking into his eyes and willing her own to stay dry she said,

"Oh, Andrew you are the most wonderful man in the

whole wide world. You have just made up my mind about Mary Kate. If I can see her every year then she will be happier here with the three people who love her most."

"Are you sure Maura?"

"I'm very sure. That doesn't mean that I won't grieve for her. But I know that I must put her best interests first."

"I know one thing for sure darling. You will have made three people up in that old house very happy," he said gently as he wiped the tears from her eyes.

When Sara had cleared away the dinner dishes she stole upstairs and sat silently beside Mary Kate's bed as she slept. The moon glinting through a gap in the curtain threw a silver glow onto the old rocking horse. She could smell whiffs of lavender in the air, a strange feeling that she was not alone made her look around the room. But she could only see emptiness; still the feeling persisted. She held out her hands as if to catch something, or to hold something, while at the same time feeling a great sense, of peace sweep over her. Then she kissed Mary Kate gently on the cheek and went back down to the dining room.

When they had finished their coffee Maura followed her mother out to the kitchen. She kicked the big door shut behind her, then putting the empty cups on the table she turned to Sara.

"Mother. I want you to be the first to know, that I've decided that Mary Kate would be happier here with you."

"Oh, darling, darling, I can't tell you how much that means to me. You have made the right decision," she said, throwing her arms around her.

"Always tell her that I love her very, very much."

"I will. I will always let her know that you love her."

Chapter 19

Donegal 1947

James Thompson took his place at the window in the sitting room to wait for Mary Kate. Glancing at the clock he sighed to himself, for he knew that she wouldn't arrive for at least half an hour. This was, her first term in college, and he had missed her more than he would ever have believed possible. From the kitchen he could smell the delightful aromas of Christmas. He wondered again about what he would have done without Sara, strong, kind understanding Sara. Turning a somber gaze down the driveway, his thoughts went back over the nineteen years since Sara and Mary Kate came into his life.

He was somehow managing to live a day at a time without alcohol since his stroke fifteen years ago, the memory of which still made him shudder; the sudden violent headache, and then the terrible realisation that he was paralysed down his right side. He remembered the humiliation of having to be lifted and laid; having to be lifted on to the commode was the worst indignity of all. He had pleaded with Sara to end it for him; instead she brought Mary Kate. He remembered her sitting on the bed and caressing his head with her wee soft chubby hands.

"Will you make me a wheel-barrow when you're better Uncle James?" she had asked. In that instant he could feel the stirrings of the will to fight his way back. Now only a slight gait in his walk was the only evidence of his stroke.

In the lowering light of the leaden afternoon he painfully remembered his wasted drunken years, when life passed him by in intoxicated stupor's. There had been a war of independence, and a civil war in Ireland, and it all seemed to have passed him by. He remembered having been picked up by the black and tans one winter night. They had questioned him about the I.R.A. for half an hour, until the sergeant said, "he is just a drunken bum," then he was thrown from the wagon at the side of a dark laneway.

'It would hardly qualify me as a historian,' he thought wryly.

Jean's death five years earlier had hit him hard, he still missed her an awful lot. But she was ninety, three years old, he reminded himself. She had succumbed to heart failure in the end and died peacefully in Sara's arms. 'What we would all have done without you Sara, I'll never know,' he whispered. Getting up stiffly from his position at the window, he climbed the stairs, then walking along the landing he opened the door of what had been the locked room, and stood looking around for a moment. Sara had done a grand job in getting it into shape. Going over to the fireplace, he carefully put a few, turf on the fire and left the room and went back down to the window again to wait.

He was barely seated when he heard the engine, and the car loomed out of the gloom. Going out into the hallway he yelled to Sara, "she's here, she's here!"

Sara came running out of the kitchen removing her apron as she went. From the doorway they watched a tall beautiful smiling Mary Kate get out of the car. She ran and hugged them in turn again and again. "I've missed you two so much, so very much."

"Not half as much as we have missed you I am willing to bet," Sara said.

"Come in and get warmed up, and tell us all about college. Remember we want to hear everything. And when you have had something to eat, I have a surprise for you," James added.

"Spoiling me again already," Mary Kate said smiling up at him. "Why of course. We have been waiting to do just that."

When they had eaten and the flurry of excitement about her homecoming died down James said,

"Come with me, I have something to show you."

She followed him up the stairs and along the landing. When he opened the door of the usually locked room she was mystified.

"This is your room from now on Mary Kate," he said. Looking around the beautiful restored room, Mary Kate was lost for words; he was giving her the one room in the house that she knew held his happiest memories, and which he guarded as his special shrine to her memory. Her gaze went to the portrait.

"I was going to remove it. But your grandmother said no," he said quietly.

"Do you think she would approve?"

"I know she would approve."

Turning around she looked at him with love and affection in her eyes. She walked over to where he stood and rested her head against the rough surface of his old tweed jacket.

"Thank you Uncle James. You couldn't have paid me a greater honour."

"It is my greatest pleasure. And I have something else to tell you now that we are alone. I have made a will, and I am leaving the house to your grandmother and then to you, after your grandmother's day.

"I don't know what to say. I can't bear to think of you dying. You have meant the world to me for as long as I can remember. Are you sure?"

"I'm sure. And as for dying, we all have to do that someday. In fact I have lived longer than I deserve," he said, with his usual wry self- depreciating humour.

Her next question startled him.

"Are you my father? Every time I bring up the topic, my grandmother changes the subject." Stepping back he looked at her for a few seconds before he answered.

"I wish I was your biological father Mary Kate. But I feel like I am your father in every other sense. I love you dearly."

"Will you tell me who my father is then?" she asked, with a note of urgency in her voice. As he gazed at her lovely young face, he knew that he could not tell her that her father was an evil rapist who preyed on children.

He sighed deeply and gestured her to sit in the chair by the window, then he sat down opposite her. "Mary Kate," he began. "I didn't know your father, but I knew of him. It seems he was a neighbour and a second cousin of your mother's. They didn't love each other. You could er...say that he took advantage of your... her. She was little more than a child herself, when you came along. But, she loved you dearly from the moment you were born as did your grandmother, and later Jean and myself joined the ranks."

She sat silently not taking her steady gaze from his face, then she asked,

"is he still alive?"

"That I can't answer. I don't suppose he will ever know now what a wonderful treasure he missed out on in you. For that reason alone, I pity him."

She sat motionless not taking her eyes from his face, then she asked. "Uncle James can I call you father from now on?" Reaching across, he took her hand in his as a broad smile crossed his face making it suddenly magnificent. Then he said, "nothing in the whole world would give me greater pleasure."

Two days before Christmas Mary Kate got a letter from her mother. When she finished reading it her face lit up.

"We are all going to the U.S.A. in the spring, all three of us. Look I have the tickets," she shrieked excitedly.

"I'm delighted for you love. But don't you think that we are a bit long in the tooth for traipsing half way round the world."

"No you're not. Anyhow, I'm not going without you, so there. You can both start getting your glad rags gathered up when Christmas is over," she ordered, with a mischievous glint in her eyes.

They both smiled at her indulgently, then Sara said, "I suppose if God spares us, maybe we could at least give it some thought." Then looking across at James she saw him nod.

Chapter 20

New York 1948

Maura lay in the darkness listening to Andrew's familiar heavy breathing. Turning over she touched his hair gently, and her heart was filled with love for him.

They had weathered the successive catastrophes that had befallen them during their fifteen years marriage, and the wall- street crash that almost ended his business empire. His brother David was devastated and tragically ended his own life. His empire had been his whole world, and he felt that he could not face life without it. She still remembered the pain his mother went through and how she felt helpless in her efforts to comfort her. She also saw the misery in Andrew's eyes, the signs of weariness and strain, and the lost look.

During the five years that followed, life was very difficult financially, and difficult emotionally.

As she lay sleepless she thought it strangely ironic that Quinn Laughlin had seen them through the worst financial ravages of the hungry Thirties.

Hannah had brought bales of dressmaking material at a bankruptcy sale, and produced cheap practical clothing for her former wealthy clients. Maura had worked in the shop right up until Andrew junior's birth, and after his birth she took him to the shop with her. She had continued to work until James was born, at which point they were once again on the road to financial security again. Now here she was waiting to see the daughter that she hadn't seen for fifteen years, and she was both excited and scared. Getting out of bed quietly she went to the sitting room, and watched dawn break in the eastern sky. Andrew's voice startled her.

"Are you all right sweetheart? Heard you get up," he said, sitting down on the sofa next to her.

"I'm fine. Just a wee bit anxious about today."

"I have always felt guilty about you not seeing your family for all these years. No one could have foretold what was ahead of us back then I suppose," he sighed taking her hand in his. Smiling up at him she said with emotion in her voice. "Andrew you are the best thing that ever happened to me. You weren't responsible for the depression or the war.
With the help of God, we will have enough years left to make up for lost time. Now I must go and get the boys up," she said smiling tenderly.

David junior tried to protect himself, emotionally with the armour of the young. But Maura knew how much he had suffered in silence; rejected by his mother and in his mind also by his father. Andrew and she had tried to make it up to him in every way possible. He had grown into a tall good- looking youth. Maura looked at her two sons and at David with pride as they stood excitedly waiting for the ship to dock.

"Can you see them yet?" David asked. Maura shook her head and continued to stare at the sea of faces lining the decks. Then she saw her mother and waved up at her while tears stung her eyes and her throat ached with relief.

When they finally emerged from the ship Maura had only eyes for the beautiful stranger that was her daughter, and her, generous heart grieved for all the absent years. She studied the face so much like her own before walking forward with her arms outstretched.

"Mary Kate, I'm so glad you're here," she said emotionally as she hugged her.

Mary Kate smiled shyly at this woman who was her mother, and yet a stranger to her.

Then turning to Sara they embraced each other joyfully.

"I'm so glad to see you; so very glad Maura. Now I want to meet my grandsons." Maura watched a little sadly as her sons greeted their grandmother formally. Then over her Mothers shoulder Maura saw James standing alone in the background. Going over to where he stood she held out her hand. "Welcome," she said quietly. Then she leant forward and kissed him on the cheek.

" The years have been kind to you Maura. Have you been happy?"

"I couldn't have been happier James. And I will forever be in your debt for all the happy years with Andrew." Smiling down at her he squeezed her hand.

The following days passed slowly and pleasantly enough, as they all settled into the task of getting to know each other. Mary Kate felt shy and ill at ease in her Mother's company, although Maura was trying very hard to make up for lost time; trying too hard perhaps she thought. It was with a sense of sadness that Mary Kate realised that it was too late for them ever to be really close as Mother, and daughter.

In spite of her best efforts not to Maura found, herself again studying Mary Kate for signs of any resemblance to Seamus. But to her great relief she saw none. She thought she had succeeded in putting him out of her mind for good, and she hated herself for letting thoughts of him trouble her mind again.

David and Mary Kate sat on the park bench silently watching the boys play ball.

"I can't get used to having young brothers. I suppose I've been alone for too long". Mary Kate said quietly.

" I know what you mean. I was ten when I came to live with Uncle Andrew and aunt Maura."

"Is your mother still alive?" Maura asked.

"Yes as far as I know. I haven't seen her for four years or more. She was never really interested in me you see," he said earnestly. Then looking straight ahead he added, "neither was my father for that matter. He was more interested in making money than fatherhood. I don't think he gave me a thought when he committed suicide when the crash came."

Mary Kate looked at his face and quickly looked away again, not knowing what to say to him. Then she said quietly,

"I'm sorry."

"Oh, don't be sorry. I'm happy now, I've put all that behind me," he said smiling at her.

In the distance Mary Kate saw her grandmother and James slowly making their way towards them along the path. She could feel her heart lighten and fill up with love at sight of them. Suddenly she realised what a charmed life filled with love that she had led; and all because of these two special human beings. As she watched them come closer she remembered old Molly singing her to sleep away back in the distant past, and later Jean Thompson's love and kindness was etched on her earliest memories.

She smiled at them as they came up to the beach. James slumped down beside her.

"This heat is a bit much for me. Not used to it I suppose." he said.

Mary Kate thoughts went back to the grey house on the cliff, and to her room overlooking the sea that she had recently made her own, and she knew instantly that it was the only place that would always be her home.

Knowing who her father was didn't seem to matter to her anymore; James Thompson had earned the right to be all, the father that she needed.

Studying James' face for a few seconds Mary Kate asked,

"Father, is it all right if I invite David to Ireland for a holiday next year?"

With a broad smile of pleasure he said, "daughter of mine, nothing would give me greater pleasure."

FOR LOVE OF MARY KATE